STEREOTYPE

Also by Claire Hennessy

Memories
Dear Diary
Being Her Sister

Published by Poolbeg

STEREOTYPE

CLAIRE HENNESSY

POOLBEG
FOR CHILDREN

ABOUT THE AUTHOR

Claire Hennessy is a seventeen-year-old who prefers to avoid reality, hence her love of writing. She is currently attending Loreto Beaufort and lives in Dublin.

Visit her at *www.clairehennessy.com*

Published 2003
by Poolbeg Press Ltd
123 Grange Hill, Baldoyle
Dublin 13, Ireland
E-mail: poolbeg@poolbeg.com

1 3 5 7 9 10 8 6 4 2

A catalogue record for this book is available from the British
Library.

ISBN 1-84223-165-0

Typeset by Magpie Designs in Palatino 12pt / 16.3pt
Printed by Cox & Wyman Ltd, Reading, Berkshire

www.poolbeg.com

For Maeve

ACKNOWLEDGEMENTS

The author would like to thank
the following people who kept her
from going (more) insane during
the writing of this book. These
include her kind, loving parents
who make tea and remind her to
sleep and that sort of thing, her
cat, her brother, her computer
(What? It's almost a person!),
her friends (in particular Paula,
Andrew, Jenny, Claire, Darragh,
Garóg, Nazuma and Maeve),
her relatives (in particular the
rather wacky McBrearty clan),
her teachers, various people at
school (in particular the S class),
the people at Poolbeg Press and,
of course, the readers.

Always remember you're unique.
Just like everyone else.

Chapter One

I can't help feeling that I'm a slave to consumerism.
I mean, whenever I'm depressed, I buy *stuff. Stuff*
makes me happy. It's usually something that I
could have lived without - a CD that I only half-
like, a book I'll read once and then forget about, a
top I'm never going to wear - but in the moment,
when there's you and there's this "blah" feeling
and a dark cloud hanging over your head, it
doesn't matter. It's about buying something,
acquiring some new item to add to the collection.
It's about filling the empty gap in your life with
something tangible.

In fairness, it probably beats my other method of

combating the blahness and the emptiness, which involves playing around with razor-blades and leaves thin red scabs running along the underside of my left arm.

Cue your rolling of eyes, or disgust, or shock and horror, or whatever. And what are your emotions towards our protagonist now? Choose from the options below . . .

a) Oh, what a troubled young woman she must be.

b) Attention-seeking brat with no concept of how hard real life *really* is.

c) So what? It's not like you're the only one who does it. Quit making a big deal out of it.

Yeah, I probably am an attention-seeker. I'll admit that. It's not like I cut that often, but when I started doing it, last summer, it was purely to get sympathy and concern and attention and recognition. I thought, OK, maybe Sarah will see this and she'll ask me what's wrong, or Graham will notice and he'll demand an explanation, or *something*. But I think even if that had happened, I would have shrugged and said, "Nothing. I'm OK. Everything's fine." Like I always do. So I wore long sleeves until the marks stopped being so noticeable. The scabs fall off after about a week, and even though there's sometimes a line left on the skin, it's not dramatic enough to spot, unless you're looking for it.

The reason I keep doing it is because it *works* - for a brief while, anyway. In Third Year we discussed in one class, probably Home Ec or Health Ed or something, why people would want to hurt themselves and, although I stayed silent, I was thinking, 'It's so obvious! You hurt because it's easier to deal with physical pain than emotional pain.' And it's true. Make yourself hurt, make your arm bleed, and it takes your mind off whatever's bothering you. Of course it's only temporary. Just like stuff. Once you've bought it and come down from that purchasing-goods high, you're back to where you started.

I'm on an endless pursuit of happiness. I've tried not eating, eating, boys, good grades, being bitchy, books and CDs, clothes, sport, writing poetry, cutting . . . nothing seems to work as a long-term solution. What I want is a quick fix. A sachet of Instant Joy. Just add water, and you're set for life. Too bad the world doesn't seem to work that way.

Yeah, I'm lazy. Yeah, I don't want to work at making my life bearable. Who does?

It's not like I have any big excuse for being like this. I wish I did. I wish there was a reason, something I could pin down and exclaim triumphantly, "That's it! *That's* why I feel like this!" I tried suggesting to my mom that she take me to a psychologist to see if I could be analysed, in the hope that maybe I was actually clinically depressed and could be treated, but she dismissed the idea. If only I had some childhood trauma, something or someone to blame. But no. What I have are two parents (still together, cordial if not passionately devoted to one another), a younger sister (a rocker whose given name is Jessica Marie Evans but who is going through a phase of answering only to JM as she thinks it "sounds cooler"), and a younger brother (a football fanatic named Greg). We are not a dysfunctional family. We are boringly *normal*. My dad has even got involved with coaching the local under-eleven team, which Greg is on. He's become one of those involved-in-the-community, helpful-volunteer-type people. I hate it.

I never want to have kids. Never, ever. I know, I know. You're smirking to yourself right now thinking, "She says that now . . . but she'll be married at twenty-five and burdened down by children by the time she's thirty. I bet. Just wait and see." And maybe you're right. Maybe in a couple of years I'll get broody and decide that the one thing that will complete my life will be a child. It's scarily possible, actually. A baby will be the newest item on my list for whatever will make me happy.

But I never want to be one of those people whose identity disappears once they have children and they become nothing more than a *parent*. No longer an individual with thoughts and hopes and opinions and dreams - just a mother nagging at the kids to keep their rooms tidy and to do their homework and to wear a jacket out because it's cold.

If I grow up to be my mother, I want someone to shoot me. Sarah can probably be persuaded into doing it. As the girl who tapes *ER* for her every week, I deserve some kind of compensation.

Chapter Two

Monday morning. Sarah is not going into school as she is "sick", her mom informs me. Roughly translated, that means she didn't feel like facing double Physics today. She misses an awful lot of Mondays.

I usually walk to school with her because she lives on my road and because I don't get to see her during classes. She's in Fifth Year, and I'm a lowly Transition Year, so the only time I see her during the day is when we walk. Karen lives nearby as well, but she gets a lift in every morning, even though it's only a ten-minute walk. In a way I'm sort of glad. Karen's nice, I guess, but she's in almost every single one of my classes and too much of her is definitely a bad thing.

It feels like the weekend didn't really happen. Like it was just five minutes ago that Sarah, Karen,

Fiona and me collectively sagged with relief as we left school on Friday afternoon and went to watch videos at Fiona's for the evening. Like Saturday in town was just a dream, as was my Sunday spent at home curled up with new books. It never really happened. The concept of a weekend doesn't actually exist. We just come to school, go home, sleep, come to school, go home, sleep, come to school . . .

Karen is already there by the time I arrive, perched on a table in one corner of the classroom, where our usual group has congregated. I get a few half-hearted "Hi"s when I join them. It's OK, guys, you don't have to acknowledge me, really.

Hannah over there - you can ignore me, it's fine. I don't really care if you don't realise I exist.

Remember that episode of *Buffy* where the girl becomes invisible because as far as everyone's concerned, she is? That'll be me someday. Only sometimes I wish I were invisible. I want to disappear . . . I don't want anyone to see me, because when they see you, they can judge you.

Leanne, sitting next to Hannah, is the sort of person you *don't* want to realise that you're alive. She's sarcastic. She's bitchy. She makes you feel about two inches tall. Standing up to her abuse means she'll just attack you even more. If you want to stay friends with her, stay in the circle, keep quiet.

Stereotype

I can't believe I used to be friends with her. I can't believe I used to think the way she does. I can't believe the fact that while I've managed to change from a spoiled, obnoxious brat completely uncaring of how other people feel, she's still exactly the same.

Karen gets on with her. Karen is the sort of person who appears comfortable in any situation, around any group of people. In other words, the exact opposite to me.

It's weird, though. Sometimes I find myself not caring about what they all think of me, and other times I'm hurt that they don't want me around. At the very least, they don't care whether I'm there or not. I don't matter to them.

No, I'm not looking for sympathy or pity from you, thank you very much. I mean, it's not like I go home crying about how I don't fit into their perfect little teenager lives. I barely think about them. I don't *want* to fit in. Not really. I don't want to be like them. I don't want to turn into a condescending, superficial bitch. I don't want my life to revolve around drinking and partying and meeting fellas.

I just . . . I want to be *out* of here, you know? I want to be in college, studying something I'm really interested in. I want to meet interesting people who'll understand me. I want to be able to wear my own clothes the whole time instead of a sickening

7

uniform. I want to be cool and confident in an off-beat kind of way, I want people to like me, I want to be out there in the real world instead of stuck here in an all-girls school where being shallow and fake is as much a part of the daily routine as racing through your homework five minutes before the class starts.

Maybe I'm fooling myself. Maybe college isn't the Utopia I would like it to be. Maybe it's going to be as hellish as school is.

Tina's going on about her diet and how much she needs to lose weight. I tune out. Otherwise I'll have to kill her. I mean, seriously kill her. I'd lean over and rip her head off her shoulders, then kick it around the classroom. I'd chop her arms and legs into tiny pieces. It wouldn't be pretty. So I try to ignore what she's saying.

OK, maybe she really *does* think she's too fat, but does she have any idea how insulting to other people it is to have her moaning about it? I mean, does that self-centred cow realise how offensive it is for people like me, who are of average weight, to hear her complain that she is too fat when she could rival Kate Moss in the skinniness stakes? I hate her. I really do. (Tina, not Kate Moss.)

I'm so angry with her right now. I don't care if she looks into the mirror and sees a gelatinous blob - the reality is that she is thin, and that when people like her see themselves as overweight, it makes everyone else feel pretty shitty.

Not that she even cares. All she wants is to be told that she's skinny a couple of hundred times. Then, with her ego stroked and her self-esteem boosted, she can shut up.

I surreptitiously begin pinching at the skin on my left wrist. I dig the nails in firmly each time, until I'm a little less pissed off with her, a little calmer.

After all, we don't want a scene. Sometimes I imagine what it'd be like - me having this big confrontation with someone in the class. Take your pick. On a bad day any one of them could be my worst enemy. But it'd end badly. I know. Maybe I am just a tiny bit concerned about appearances after all. Or maybe I just want to stay invisible. That way you can't get hurt.

Chapter Three

Very few people have any inkling of what goes on inside my head and I think the world is better off not knowing.

I doubt Sophie Bradley would be enthused to hear that right now I want to kill her. Seriously. If I had a gun, she'd be lying on the carpet in a spreading pool of blood and I'd be in the principal's office getting yelled at for making a mess. ("Abigail Evans, do you realise how much it will cost to get that stain out? You're in serious trouble here. I'm going to give you . . . detention.") As it is, she's sitting at the back of the classroom talking about some meaningless event in her moronic, alcohol-drenched, smoke-enveloped life. We're watching a video for English (to later analyse and deconstruct and try to sound deep and meaningful while doing so) but Sophie keeps muttering away in that trashy accent of hers. She tries so hard to sound tough and inner-city-ish. Rough is *in*, pronouncing the ends of your words is *out*. It's so pathetic. We live on the south side of the city. Deal with it.

I can *hear* the video if I try hard enough, but you know the way it is when your attention is drawn to something and you start to get annoyed about it. You block out everything else and, without meaning to, you find yourself only being able to hear the inane babbling of a bleached-blonde bimbo. Come to think of it, her dark roots are showing. Maybe I should mention it. Maybe if I don't she won't notice it, it'll grow out and then she'll manage to look halfway normal. Why does everyone think blonde is so attractive, even if it clashes hideously with their skin tone?

Oh, wait, I forgot. I go to a school which is comprised of brainless idiots. Of course.

It's not that I hate *everyone* in the entire school. Just most of them. But they're all so clichéd and utterly unoriginal, and they bore me.

Their world revolves around boys and alcohol and going out.

My world revolves around trying not to be a stereotypical misfit of an adolescent and fearing desperately that I *am*, poetry, observing human behaviour, daydreaming and music.

They want to look like Britney.

I want to write like Sylvia Plath.

You see the difference.

The last time I could honestly say I didn't hate anyone in the school was a couple of years ago, when our year got the meningitis inoculation. The pre-injection group were anxious about the thought of a needle being jabbed in their arms and the post-injection group were nauseous and tired.

Everyone was vulnerable and because of that, because of the usual barriers having disintegrated, everyone got along. People were sympathetic and caring and warm. It was incredible.

The next day the barriers were back up and everyone was as self-centred and false as they usually are.

I wasn't surprised.

Chapter Four

Well done, Abi, I tell myself as the bell goes. (The bell being a symbolic representation of the hold that the school and its rigid timetable has over all its pupils. Naturally.) I got through a whole class without storming down to the back of the class to strangle Sophie with my bare hands.

I must be maturing. You know you're really an adult when you can resist the urge to murder someone who the world would really be better off without.

In Irish we are debating the age-old question. To have or not to have a school uniform? Are they a good idea, or bad? Answers only in that archaic and hated language, please.

Louise doodles on her homework journal beside me while I scribble down what's being written on the board. Might as well *try* to learn something in school, after all.

The fairly obvious points about school uniforms are coming up. I'm not surprised. It's the fairly obvious people that are speaking up.

And what is our anti-heroine's opinion on school uniforms, you might wonder?

Does she embrace the idea of everyone being equally hideous and having each person's creativity stifled?

Or does she hate them and wish she could wear whatever she wants, just to show people that she's different?

Well, what do *you* think?

The discussion in the class is at first pro-uniform. It seems everyone absolutely loves the idea of these bright blue monstrosities. After all, without them we'd get to be individuals and we wouldn't want that, would be? They don't. They want to be identical. They're terrified of being different.

Idiots! Don't they get it? Normality is *boring*. They're boring.

If we didn't have to wear a uniform I'd dress all in black and dye my hair bright purple. Or I'd wear long denim skirts and T-shirts with slogans like "Nobody knows I'm a lesbian", just because it would be so much *fun* to see the reaction of the masses. Or I'd wear fishnet and lace . . . or not bother and just wear tracksuits, because it is only school after all and I'm not trying to impress anyone. Except maybe I would be - determined to stand out just to get attention.

Aren't middle children meant to be the ones who feel they have to act out to get attention? Something is clearly wrong in the Evans family dynamic. Maybe we are dysfunctional after all. I can only hope . . .

Our teacher is looking bored and asks for the

disadvantages of uniforms. Funny, I thought the teachers were meant to be brainwashing us into thinking that uniforms are a good thing. She should really stop while she's ahead.

Before you know it, the class is spouting out pro-individuality propaganda, and discussing how much they hate the uniform. Anyone who is still in favour of the idea is silenced by the mob, and by the time the bell goes I know exactly what side I'll be taking when we have to write a short essay on our views on uniforms for homework.

School uniforms: definitely a good idea. How could you possibly think otherwise?

Chapter Five

The sad truth is that I wish I were like them sometimes.

Not the whole alcohol-is-the-centre-of-my-existence-matched-only-by-boys-and-clothes attitude.

Or the I'm-such-a-rebel-because-I-listen-to-the-type-of-alternative-music-that's-so-trendy-and-commercialised-that-I'm-really-not-being-rebellious-at-all-but-just-following-the-crowd kind of way.

Just the easy friendship they seem to have, the teenage normality that they all take for granted, that I used to imagine I'd have when I finally became a teenager. I should have known that turning thirteen wouldn't mean a sudden transformation into a butterfly.

I envy the pretty ones, who look beautiful effortlessly and don't even realise it, and who are *friendly* on top of it all.

And the talented ones, the artistic, the musical, the athletic, the intelligent, the dramatic, the ones who have a *gift* and don't realise that others *don't*.

And when they're pretty *and* talented, it just hurts. In the great cosmic scheme of things, a lot of things aren't fair. It's not fair that people get sick and die; it's not fair that bad things can happen to good people. And compared to those *big* issues, it seems a little childish to complain about it not being fair that people have so much going for them when you don't.

So call me childish, then!

Chapter Six

Leanne and I were best friends from fifth class onwards. We did the usual best friend stuff - talked about boys, painted each other's nails, listened to pop music together, bitched about almost everyone we knew.

I started being friends with her because she was

nice to me. She told me I was smart and that she wanted to be friends with me. I was flattered, having absolutely no self-esteem, and we began hanging out.

Neither of us were contestants for the Miss Popularity pageant. We didn't even make it through the first round. I was quiet and weird; she was bossy and mean. Maybe she did think I was cool, or maybe she just needed a friend and anyone would do. "Using" is an overused word in the primary school vocabulary, but it's probably because it happened so much. People are selfish and to be alone is unthinkable. So you use people. You mightn't even like them, but they suit your needs right now.

It doesn't automatically stop when you enter secondary school, either. Maybe not even when you head out into The Real World. Sometimes you don't even know that you're doing it, and sometimes you don't realise how much you can hurt other people. But you do it all the same. I've done it. More than once. Too often.

Maybe I was using her too. I needed a friend as much as she did. But I don't think I ever dismissed her the way she did me, making me feel like a tiny insect she wanted to crush. I *never* put her down the way she constantly did to me. She set out to make me feel stupid and inferior and it worked. Of course I probably would have felt that way anyway. I was just about as neurotic and insecure then as I am now. The only difference is I was much bitchier back then.

We were as close as sisters and fought about as much too. And eventually I started hating her. I could have entire conversations with other friends about how much I hated her. Like Hannah, who agreed with me entirely - but who was too scared of her to stand up to her.

I hated Hannah for that, for her weakness. I hated everyone who put up with being treated like crap. I spent a lot of time seething, then finally exploded into screams and tears.

I was fourteen and I'd lost my best friend of four years. Never mind that she'd been an awful friend - I was alone and lonely and miserable and I hated it. I was Angry Abi. You didn't want to be around me. I hated the world and the world hated me.

Later I learned how to be a good girl, a normal girl, and how to turn the rage inwards instead.

Chapter Seven

I don't want you to think I'm crazy. Well, *part* of me doesn't. The other part is hoping that I am. Then maybe everything would make sense.

I mean, look at my arm, for God's sake! *Look* at it!

See the red scratches and the fading scars? Now tell me that I'm perfectly OK and that everything's going to be all right. Just try it. Do you really believe what you're saying?

Oh, oh, and I'm Attention-Seeking Abi again. Sorry, I'll try to stop myself from doing that, but it's hard when you spend a great deal of your time feeling like you're screaming into a void.

It's weird because I really hate people who are always whining on and on and on about their problems. Even Fiona and Karen can get on my nerves sometimes. Sarah is the exception to the rule because I trust her completely. There's a lot she doesn't know about me, but she knows me better than Fiona does, better than Karen does, better than all those people at school do.

I mean, how many of them would suspect that Abigail Evans hates herself? She's too quiet to make much of an impression on anyone who doesn't make a point of getting to know her. Even then she won't reveal much. She's a relatively good student. She doesn't do any sports but she doesn't mind PE, although her laziness leads to her just not bothering with it most of the time. She lends CDs to her friends and daydreams a lot. She scribbles quotes from songs and poems on her homework journal amid various squiggles and doodles. She sometimes talks about herself in the third person, which is probably just a way for her to distance herself from her disturbed psyche.

Disturbed psyche? God, who even *talks* like that? No wonder I'm so completely introverted. I'm weird. I'm the stereotypical school nerd/outcast/freak (tick all boxes that apply, and they all do).

I don't want to be a stereotype. I just want to be me.

Chapter Eight

Fiona is in the library when I go up there at lunchtime to bring back a book that has been overdue for about three years. (Yep. I'm one of those scary people who visit libraries regularly. Oh come *on*, don't tell me you're surprised. You knew it was coming.)

"Hey," she smiles at me.

"Hey," I return. "What're you looking for?"

"History stuff. We have this essay to do, and we're meant to get 'extra sources'. I hope they have something here."

"When d'you have to have it done for?"

She checks her watch. "About two hours from now?"

I grin. "I see."

She shrugs. "I know, I know. I'm hopeless." She takes a book off the shelf and flicks through it.

"Yeah, this'll do. Hey, did Sarah tell you about her band?"

"Her *what*?"

She laughs. "Yeah, I know. She wants to set up a band."

I am in shock. "Why?"

Fiona shrugs. "Don't ask me. She thinks it's going to be cool. She was talking to this guy Shane yesterday, who plays the guitar - he suggested the idea, and she fell in love with it."

"Or him," I mutter.

"Probably! She's really excited about the idea, anyway."

Silence. Huh. I never really know what to say around Fiona when it's just the two of us, because I don't know her that well. She's more Sarah's friend than mine - they're in the same class - and since I am not Karen and therefore *not* always at ease with people, we have an awkward silence.

"I'd better go write that essay," Fiona smiles.

"Good luck," I smile back.

Back in the classroom I sit on a desk and swing my legs while the group babble on about last weekend (party at someone's house) and next weekend (St Patrick's Day is on Monday, so there are various activities going on). I am still in shock at the thought of Sarah being in a band.

You see, Sarah is even less enthusiastic than I am

about things. She is one of those people who can barely find the energy to do PE and go to her piano lessons every week, let alone be part of a band. She loves music, sure, but I just can't see her in a band. It's such a clichéd thing to do, the alternatively-trendy hobby. *Everyone* seems to be in a band or know someone who is. It's so . . . un-Sarah-like.

You know that awful disconcerted feeling you get when you realise that something you've taken for granted turns out to be completely wrong, and that you don't know one of your best friends as well as you thought you did? Or maybe even at all? That's me now.

Maybe it's just that she likes this Shane guy, and wants to get to know him better. But that idea is even weirder than the first. She wouldn't go to all that trouble for some boy, even if it was, say, Brad Pitt. (Well, maybe for Brad Pitt, but since I don't *think* he's lurking around Dublin posing as a seven-teen-year-old guitar player, it's not really an issue.)

My world has suddenly stopped making any sense whatsoever.

Chapter Nine

On the way home I listen to Alanis Morissette on my Walkman. 'Hands Clean' is an obsession of mine. Karen stopped liking her because she thought she was getting too "popular" and commercialised, but I think that it's just part of her "I can't like anything remotely popular or something that isn't completely and utterly obscure" phase. I hate that. Why can't people just listen to what they want to without being defined by it? Oh, but wait. Then we'd all have to judge people on what they're *really* like instead of having neat categories that everyone slots into. We couldn't have that.

Greg is out playing football with his friends; Jess is probably listening to horrendously loud "music" at someone's house. I have the house to myself.

I switch on the computer, open a blank Microsoft Word file and stare at it for a few minutes before closing it and going to watch TV instead.

Sometimes you just can't write, even when you've been meaning to. Besides, I have nothing to say. Except perhaps *Oh, how strange this all is/ Sarah is starting a band!* Nope. Definitely not the beginnings of an epic masterpiece.

There is nothing on TV. Well, obviously there's *something*, but nothing worth watching. I turn on my phone. One message from Sarah. *Not going 2 school 2day, c u later.* I'll go around to her house and if she's not too "sick" to see me, I'll ask her what the story is with this band idea.

I used to want to be a singer. Famous and beautiful and adored universally, with little girls dreaming of being just like me when they grew up. Then I realised that not only am I not beautiful, but I have no musical ability whatsoever. I love listening to it, but as far as being creative in that area goes, I'm a hopeless failure.

Sarah writes songs. I found that out the first day I actually spoke to her. She doesn't often show me her stuff, just like I tend to keep anything I write to myself, but sometimes she will. I guess I'm a little jealous. It's not fair that she's so talented when it comes to music. I'd hate her if she wasn't as insecure as I am.

And now I'm more than a little jealous. This whole new musical world has opened up to her, a world where she and Shane and assorted others will live in harmony (ouch, bad pun) and where I'll be lucky to be invited for occasional visits.

She hasn't even gone through the door yet, but already I'm worrying and paranoid about our friendship. Just call me Abigail "Overreacting" Evans . . .

Chapter Ten

I know Sarah's room almost as well as I know my own. Around her mirror she has a bunch of those cool fridge magnets, the ones that have great phras-

es on them like When I found Mr Right I didn't realise his first name was Always. Fiona bought that one for her after she broke up with Kieran, her boyfriend of six months. None of us, including Sarah, was too broken-hearted when that relationship ended. In fact, as I recall, we went out to Planet Hollywood to celebrate.

"Hey, guess what?" Sarah says.

"You're starting a band," I reply.

She looks disappointed at not getting to announce it. "Fiona told you, yeah?"

"Yeah."

"So . . ."

"So . . . what?"

"So what do you *think*?" she demands.

"Does it really matter what I think?" I ask.

"Abi! Yeah, it does. You think it's a stupid idea, don't you?"

Honesty is the best policy, but also helps you lose friends quicker than any other virtue.

"No! I think it'll be great," I lie.

"Really?" she beams.

"Really. Come on, tell me more about it."

"You sure? I don't want to bore you to death."

I don't want her to bore me to death either, but she has this gigantic smile on her face and is bubbling with energy and excitement. I hope it's not infectious.

"Just tell me," I say.

"Well, I ran into Shane yesterday. You know Shane, right?"

I shrug. "I don't think so."

"You *do* . . . he remembers you, anyway. I used to work with him in Superquinn. He came over here a couple of times."

While I am still musing over whether I can recall Shane or not, Sarah continues.

"Well, he's still there, and I saw him yesterday, and we started talking about music and stuff. He called around when he finished work and we decided - we're going to start a band."

"I hear he's a guitar player, huh?"

"Yep. And he writes songs, and sings, and - he's just so talented, Abi, you would not believe it."

I grin. "You like him, don't you?"

She shrugs sheepishly. "Maybe a little. I don't know. But it's more just . . . oh, I don't know. He likes all the same bands that I do, and we just - see music the same way. It's amazing."

I can't remember the last time she sounded this happy. I mean, she's normally cheerful, but *this* - this I don't think I've ever seen before.

"That's great," I say honestly.

"Yeah . . . it is." She beams again and twirls around the room. "I can't wait until we get started. Shane has a couple of friends who might be interested. And I've been writing new songs all day. It's like - now I have a *reason* for writing them. It's just - incredible." She laughs. "So, any news with you?"

Well, Sarah, although I'm delighted that you've found a purpose to your life, I'm just a teeny bit jealous of your happiness and will probably go home after this and play with sharp objects.

I shrug. "Not really, no."

Chapter Eleven

This year at school has been full of irrelevant, pointless activities. I suppose if I had thrown myself into it I would have gotten more out of it, but as you know, I'm lazy. It was a nice idea back in September, the thought of me enthusiastically Getting Involved in as much as possible, but I never put it into practice.

It's almost over, though. I mean, it's mid-March. We get our Easter holidays in a couple of weeks and then it's just a matter of biding our time until the summer holidays. I can't wait.

Then, Fifth Year. Actual work. I'm not sure how I'll cope, but I have a feeling it'll involve a lot of chanting to myself, "Just another two years and you're out of here."

It is Tuesday and we all have a morning of Irish

dancing. Apparently some nutcase in the staff-room thought it would be a good idea to subject our year to this torture. Tragically, my tracksuit and runners are at home. I try to look distraught as I explain the situation to the teacher. I am sent off to be supervised along with assorted others, including Caroline, a fellow survivor of Junior Cert German. I sat beside her for three years and we bonded in hatred for the subject. Needless to say, we're not planning on continuing with it for the Leaving.

"Hey," I say, sitting down beside her.

"Hey. Not doing Irish dancing, huh?"

"No."

"You must be heartbroken."

"I am," I grin, pretending to wipe away a tear. "But I'll cope."

"I bet. Have a good weekend?"

"It was OK. How about you?"

"Same. I was working all day Saturday."

"Fun."

"Oh yeah. There was one girl who came in looking for the Mandy Moore album and threw a fit when she realised we didn't have it. She actually started screaming at me because it wasn't in the shop."

"Oh my God. How old was she?"

"About ten," Caroline rolls her eyes. "I almost

felt like yelling right back at her for having such crappy taste in music."

I laugh. OK, so I'm against judging people by what kind of music they listen to - but come *on*! No sane person would yell over Mandy Moore.

"Did we all have such bad taste when we were kids?" she sighs.

I nod. "Hate to tell you, but . . . yeah."

She smiles. "At least we recovered."

"True."

Pause. "I still listen to Britney, though," she confesses sheepishly.

"I bought the latest Westlife album," I admit.

We laugh.

"This conversation never happened," I say.

"What conversation?" she asks innocently.

Chapter Twelve

I'd love to be pretty. I wonder what it feels like, to be able to look in the mirror and beam at your reflection. Sure, I have my good days, the days when I feel that I don't need to put a paper bag over my head. But there's no way that I'm *pretty*.

For starters, I am not tall and willowy and graceful, or petite and cute and delicate. I'm somewhere in between. Same with my figure - I'm not thin or fat, just average. I have freckles, but not too many of them. And my hair - oh, my hair.

Ever read *Anne of Green Gables*? You know the way she's completely distraught over the fact that her hair is red? Well, that's me. I like to call it "auburn". It's grown darker in recent years, which can only be a good thing, but it's still most definitely not brown.

If I could look like any one of my friends, I'd have to pick Sarah. Fiona is actually prettier than she is, but Sarah has one of those perpetually happy faces. Even if she's depressed, she finds something to smile about, and that makes all the difference.

Karen would never win a beauty pageant. OK, I wouldn't either, I know. She's not ugly or plain - she's just average. Maybe it's just that she's been getting on my nerves lately. People always seem more attractive when you're in a good mood with them. When you're not, you project your irritation with them onto your perception of them. That's my theory, anyway.

It certainly would explain why I think the bleached-blonde look doesn't work for so many of the bitches in our year. Then again, maybe it really is just absolutely hideous.

Chapter Thirteen

Lunch. Tina is talking about what she's going to wear out this weekend. Leanne is planning how she's going to get drink. Niamh is showing everyone the text messages from her boyfriend. Karen is participating in the fascinating discussion. I am not.

I am Silent Abi. I sit. I observe. I get extremely bored. I leave.

Caroline's sitting in her classroom with her group. If I knew them better I'd go in, but I'm not the most socially adept person on the planet. I venture up to the Fifth-Year classrooms.

Fiona and Sarah are sitting at the back of the classroom. Fiona is copying Sarah's maths homework. Sarah is nibbling at a roll and sending text messages to someone. Possibly Shane. Probably Shane.

"Texting Shane?" I ask.

She looks up. "Hey, Abi. Yeah, it's Shane."

"She is *so* in love with him," Fiona grins.

Sarah rolls her eyes. "Stop. Please. I'm not."

"Yes, you *are*. It's so obvious."

"I'm not! I'm just excited about the band, that's all."

"*Sure.*"

"Go do your homework," Sarah tells her.

Fiona goes back to her maths.

"I don't like him," Sarah says firmly. "I don't."

It sounds like she's trying to convince herself of that fact, but I don't say anything.

"I believe you," I reassure her.

I hope Shane isn't going to be the sole topic of conversation for the next six months. I remember when she was going out with Kieran. At first it was, "He's so wonderful/kind/gorgeous, don't you think so? I wonder if he likes me. Do you think he likes me? No, of course he doesn't. He probably just thinks of me as a friend. Maybe he doesn't even like me as a friend! Maybe he really hates me and every time I talk to him he can't wait to get away from me . . ."

Stage Two. Budding Romance. "I think he likes me. I mean, he's been calling me every night this week. That has to mean something, right? And we're going to the cinema on Saturday. But I don't know if it's a just-as-friends thing, or if we're going to the cinema *together*. You know what I mean?"

Stage Three. Getting Together. "So, we're officially going out now! Oh my God, I can't believe it. My boyfriend, Kieran. Wow. But what if he only wants to go out with me so he can say he has a girlfriend?"

Stage Four. Jealousy and Insecurity. "We saw his ex yesterday. She's so pretty, you wouldn't believe it. And skinny. He's still friends with her, you

31

know. He was really nice to her. He probably wishes he was still with her."

Stage Five. Boredom. "It's just not exciting anymore. He's so *predictable*. I don't even bother getting dressed up for him any more. I mean, what's the point? We're like an old married couple."

Stage Six. Fighting. "I hate him. Absolutely hate him. Every time he says something, I just want to shoot him. He's so boring! He never shuts up about that stupid car he wants to buy. I mean, who cares?"

Stage Seven. Post-Break-Up Blues. "I miss him so much. Why did I break up with him? Why? He was such a great boyfriend. I'm so *stupid*!"

Stage Eight. A New Beginning. "So we're back together now. It's great! Really! Even if he's boring and I hate his friends and he spends way too much time hanging around his ex-girlfriend. This is what I want. Really."

Stage Nine. Coming To One's Senses. "Thank God that *asshole* is out of my life for good."

Not that I don't absolutely adore Sarah. I mean, she is one of my closest friends in the entire world. I just wish that the boyfriend crisis wasn't so all-consuming. It gets boring hearing about your friend's love life. Especially if your own happens to be somewhat non-existent at the time.

Stereotype

Chapter Fourteen

To be fair to Sarah, she didn't babble on about Shane all through lunch. The babbling was mostly band-related. Sort of like Michelle in *American Pie*. Fiona and I nodded and smiled like the good friends we are.

I find it hard to get enthusiastic about anything. Sometimes even going out with my friends seems like too much effort.

After lunch it's time for assorted Pointless Classes. I settle back and examine my homework journal. Behind me, Karen is whispering to Leanne. I can't believe she doesn't realise how horrible Leanne really is. I can't believe the others don't, either. I don't get why Karen is a part of their group. An enthusiastic member, I mean. I'm just the quiet one who sits there biting her nails. She likes them. She really does.

I hate her sometimes.

Our last class is careers, in which no one listens. We get handouts on different universities. I think I'll do Arts in UCD. A nice, pointless degree, right? I can study a couple of subjects I like for a few years without having to decide what I actually want to do.

I actually love careers class, even if half the time it's devoted to a lecture on the importance of having a study timetable. It's like a glimpse into the future, the post-secondary-school bliss. I can't wait.

Sophie and the Bleach Brigade are amusing themselves by asking stupid questions and then not bothering to listen to the answers. Ha. Ha. Yes, hilarious. Ever thought of doing stand-up comedy, girls? Here's a tip - *don't*.

In two and a half years' time they will be the ones with not enough points for the course they want to do, or finding dead-end jobs which will leave them bitter and hardened before they're thirty.

Now, they waste time and annoy the hell out of the rest of the class. Well, me, at least.

Must - resist - the - urge - to - strangle -

Chapter Fifteen

I am still seething when the bell goes. What I really don't need is another dose of band fever. I might end up saying something I'd regret. I don't want that to happen either.

I'm in luck. Sarah is waiting outside the classroom for me when we're finally let out (after yet another reminder of the importance of good study habits, which is *completely* relevant to Transition-Year students) with a please-don't-hate-me look on her face.

"Shane wants me to go over to his house today, so I'll be walking back there with Fiona," she says in a rush.

I shrug. "Have a good time."

"You don't mind, do you?"

"It's ten minutes. I'll cope," I smile.

She beams. "See you tomorrow."

And it's another Alanis-accompanied walk home for Abi. When you think about it, it makes sense. Angry-girl music for angry-girl Abigail. Call me the stereotype, then, but what you don't know is that there's more to me than meets the eye. I can be reasonable-girl. I can be reliable-girl. I can be contented-girl, even. I refuse to fit into any set category, so don't even *try* to stick a label on me because it'll never fully describe who I am.

You might have noticed that I have a slight problem with conformity.

But anyway. I arrive home. Turn on TV. Check phone. My life is so mundane. One message. From Graham. Cue shudder from me.

You know, before I explain about Graham I'd like to state for the record that we were never a couple. Never. Because a lot of people seem to be under the impression that he's my ex, and that's why I can't stand him.

I never went out with Graham!

Sorry. I'm still a little uptight about the situation.

Possibly because he told everyone we were going out. Possibly because people believed him. Possibly because, before he turned into such an asshole, he was actually a really good friend.

I first started hanging out with Sarah, Fiona and Karen the summer after Second Year. Actually, Karen wasn't around much that summer, between the Gaeltacht and her month in America, but when she was, she was part of the group. Anyway, it was then that we got to know Graham and a couple of his friends, Kieran being one of them. Sarah and Kieran became SarahKieran as the summer drew to a close, and feeling rather sorry for myself now that she was spending all of her time with *him*, I ended up turning to Graham for, if not comfort, then companionship.

Fast forward to the following summer. The SarahKieran unit has been permanently shattered, Sarah celebrating with a night out and Kieran "mourning" with a new girl. Graham has become a very good friend to Abi, although Abi doesn't realise that she only thinks of him as a good friend because he knows when to compliment her and make her feel validated as a worthwhile human being. The other half of the time he is using her as an unpaid therapist/devoted listener to trivial problems (let's put it this way, if he'd been born a girl he'd be the type that would bemoan the fact that they'd broken a nail) and subtly eroding her self-esteem.

Seriously. He'd make some snide comment, but me, being the emotional mess that I am, wouldn't get angry with him for it. Instead I'd feel like a bad person, a worthless person. Then he'd say something nice about me, so I'd be completely grateful to him for cheering me up and being such a good friend.

It's a dangerous trap to fall into, letting someone else control how you feel about yourself. Why do you do it? Simple. It's for the moments when they make you feel *better*.

Anyway. Summer post-Junior-Cert-trauma, everything's going wonderfully wrong. Abi feels like crap and takes up recreational arm-slicing. (She always meant to have another hobby.) Sarah fails to notice. Graham possibly does, but doesn't say anything. Actually, thinking about it, he probably didn't, because otherwise he wouldn't have wanted to go out with me. He's not good with people with problems. Complaining about his own, sure, but scars would have scared him off.

It was one day at the end of July or the start of August that he told me he loved me. I kid you not, he actually used those words. And if they hadn't been coming out of the mouth of someone I was beginning to hate, I probably would have been flattered, at the very least.

Instead I just stared blankly at him and then said, "OK."

"I'm serious," he said.

"So . . . what do you want me to say?" I glared at him. I was pissed off with him. He'd put me in an awkward situation, and I didn't like it.

"Forget it," he snapped.

And I thought that was the end of it, I really did. And when I say "it", I don't just mean the love part, I mean our entire friendship. I was *hoping* it was.

But of course it wasn't. *Then* came the stalker-like phone calls and unexpected visits to the house. And although you've probably come to the conclusion that I'm a cold-hearted bitch, I'm actually hopeless at being mean to people if they're being friendly towards me. I mean, Graham was getting on my nerves with his fake "I really value our friendship" line, but I couldn't yell at him for it. I just couldn't.

I suspect his text message says something along those lines. Let's see . . . oh, I was right. *Abi, I miss having u 2 talk 2, ur such a good friend. Call r txt soon. Graham.*

I consider it, and scroll down through the options. Reply. Forward. Ah, there we go.

Delete.

Stereotype

Chapter Sixteen

You can probably understand why Graham isn't exactly my favourite person in the world. After I reluctantly agreed to be friends with him again, he took this to mean that I reciprocated his feelings.

And thought it would be appropriate to declare to all of his friends, and mine, that we were together.

Even people who weren't technically "friends" knew about it, like Leanne and Hannah and that crowd. And since Graham isn't exactly . . . the most *desirable* boy around, they found it pretty funny. You know how it goes. The biggest loser you know turns out to have a girlfriend. It makes for great gossip. Especially when the girl is that weird ex-friend of yours.

The one good thing about it was that people tended to be more surprised about *him* going out with someone than *me* going out with someone. I was, apparently, the lesser loser of the two of us.

To make matters worse, at the time the word was spreading, I was in Tyrone for a long weekend, staying with my cousin Sharon. By the time I got back, everybody knew.

I ran into Leanne in the newsagent's. "I heard about your new boyfriend," she grinned. To be fair, she was being friendly as opposed to bitchy that day.

"What?" I asked, confused, having just arrived back the night before.

"Graham, is that his name? Paul told me. He said the guy never shuts up about you."

"I'm not going out with him," I said, in complete and utter shock. I was *hoping* Paul had gotten it wrong, but at the same time it seemed like a very Graham-like thing to do.

Leanne seemed surprised. "He's been telling everyone. I always thought he was your boyfriend. He always seems to be with you."

"He's my stalker," I muttered. "I don't even like him as a friend any more."

"Know the feeling," she said. "See ya, Abi."

"See ya," I echoed.

Now, before you get all "Oh, Leanne seems like such a nice person, Abi has it all wrong about her", let me say that she clearly didn't believe me, because she never said *anything* to contradict the rumour, and still continues to refer to him as "that Graham guy, you know, Abi's ex-boyfriend". I'm not *completely* irrational.

After my encounter with Leanne I went over to Sarah's.

"Abi, what's the story? Graham's been going on about how he's madly in love with you and how great it is now that he's with you. I thought you hated him."

"I *do*. He made it up," I said quietly.

"What? Seriously? He just . . . made it up?"

I nodded. "All I told him was that I was OK with us being friends again. But apparently he, being the *freak* that he is, decided that *that* meant it was OK to lie and tell everyone we're going out."

The more I thought about it, the angrier I got, and Sarah was backing me up one hundred per cent.

"What a complete *shithead*!" she raged. "I mean, what's his *problem*, anyway? First he practically *stalks* you, then he *completely* insults you by telling everyone you're with him! Like anyone would actually *lower* themselves to his standard."

Never mind the fact that three months previously I had gushed to her about how *nice*, how *considerate* Graham was. She was kind enough not to mention it. Selective memory should be exercised among friends. Just like me conveniently forgetting about how she'd raved about Kieran a few months before when she was ranting about how awful he was.

The next day was Confrontation Day. It should have been pretty simple. I was in the right, wasn't I? I would confront him, he had no other option but to admit to being in the wrong, I would yell for a while and then leave, still angry but minus one lying bastard in my life.

41

Things didn't exactly go as planned. It was more like, I confront him; he acts puzzled and confused, denying any knowledge of these events; he then makes some stupid comment like "Why are you always so hostile?"; he follows this by accusing me of treating him badly even though he has always been there for me. *What the . . . ?*

He starts actually *listing off* occasions when I have apparently not been a good enough friend to him. I am so taken aback by this that I don't know what to say. I don't argue with him.

When he finally takes a breath I mention the fact that he makes me feel worthless. He demands examples.

Gosh, Graham, unlike you, I don't have an encyclopaedic mind which stores every single sentence ever uttered. And I certainly can't think of one offhand when you're yelling at me even though you're the liar here, you're the bad guy.

He smirks. He is triumphant. He believes himself to be the hero.

He is completely twisted.

He calls me two weeks later and says that he is willing to forgive me. I slam down the phone, but he is such a master of manipulation that I actually feel *bad* about doing it.

I hate him. More than Leanne, more than the Bleach Brigade. More than me, even.

Chapter Seventeen

Dinner in the Evans' house.

Greg: "Football. Football football. Football?"

Mom: (nodding and being an interested, involved parent)

Dad: (reads newspaper. He is the involved parent on Thursdays and Saturdays. Now he wants to catch up on the day's events.)

Greg: "Football football football."

Jess: (rolling eyes) "Shut up about your stupid football!"

Mom: (on automatic pilot) "Don't say 'shut up' to your brother."

Jess: (assuming the role of rebellious teen, since Abi is too busy rebelling by not being a rebel) "But he's boring. I don't know why you bother listening to him."

Mom: "Eat your dinner."

Jess: "You never listen to me. It's always *him*. You hate me."

Mom: "Eat your dinner."

Jess: "See? You're not even *listening* to me!"

Dad: (rolls eyes behind his newspaper)

Abi: "She can't help it. She's a middle child."

Jess: "Shut *up*! You think you know everything."

Abi: "I know more than *you* do, anyway."

Mom: "Girls, stop fighting and eat your dinner."

Abi: (wonders if her mother's preoccupation with getting them to eat their dinner is masking something deeper)

Greg: "Can I *say* something now?"

Mom: (sighing) "Go ahead."

Greg: "Football football football . . ."

Chapter Eighteen

I spend Tuesday evening online. Four new emails. One from Sarah replying to a "fill this out about me and send back" survey I sent her. Two chain-letter-type emails from Sharon. And one from Graham. He seems to be on a roll today.

I open it. It says pretty much the same thing as the text message, only with more waffling and more of a "you should feel sorry for me because my life is so horrible" vibe.

Like the text message, it gets deleted. What does he expect me to say?

Oh, yes, Graham, I'd love to be friends with you again even though you're a horrible person who enjoys manipulating other people. Interesting how, although you told me what a bad friend I was, you still cling to the idea of us being friends. By the way, I'm in a crappy mood right now and don't feel like listening to you whine about your life. I'm too self-absorbed to care about anyone but myself at the moment. Still want me to call you?

I contemplate emailing him with that message, but refrain. I'd regret it later. Graham would take it as an invitation to start ringing me regularly again.

I end up taking a bunch of online screening tests for depression. All of them say the same thing: your answers indicate you may be suffering from depression, please contact your local physician to discuss this, blah blah blah. One of them actually tells me that I am at risk for harming myself (gosh, you *think*?) and should seek immediate treatment.

I wonder if they're right. I wonder if I'm just a self-indulgent child with delusions of pain and no reason to complain.

What's so awful about my life, anyway? Everything's fine. Good family, good home, good school, good friends.

And then the things that don't fit in:

Suicidal thoughts. (Not thinking "I want to die". Just thinking about how to do it.)

Loss of appetite. (Sometimes due to earlier gorging with chocolate, but sometimes inexplicable.)

Self harm. (Most likely to get attention.)

Lack of energy. (And excessive tiredness - even though I get plenty of sleep.)

Loss of interest in once enjoyable activities. (Shopping. Phone calls to friends. Sometimes, even reading, which is quite frustrating.)

Feelings of worthlessness. (Well, I'm sixteen. It's a given.)

Maybe I'm just a neurotic teenager, and there's really nothing wrong except for the fact that I think too much. Less thinking, and more doing, is the solution.

Now, if only it didn't require so much *effort* . . .

Chapter Nineteen

Ever cried when you don't know what you're crying about? It's intense, and it's miserable, but oddly soothing at the same time. You're curled up in your bed, huddled under the duvet, and you're silently sobbing in the safety of your cocoon.

That's me, Tuesday night. I choose to blame Graham for popping up in my life again. But it's not him. Well, not entirely him. It's something that I can't quite put my finger on.

It's more than just the I-feel-so-ugly crisis and it's more than the I-hate-the-world feeling. It's like the world is right, and I'm wrong.

Ah, that's it. It's far easier to go around feeling like you're the only sane person in a bunch of crazy people. Not so easy when you start thinking that maybe you're the one who doesn't fit in.

I don't even mean fitting in at school. *That* I can handle. Not fitting in with the rest of humanity is another story.

I really should get to sleep.

Chapter Twenty

Wednesday is a bad day, filled with bad classes and bad things. Leanne is bitchy to me. Karen is too busy talking to Hannah about appropriately obscure music to notice. Sarah won't shut up about her stupid band. Even Fiona's boredom with hearing about the band is annoying me. I'm just in a disagreeable mood.

Caroline is out, so I have no one to cook with in the afternoon. Chocolate brownies are easier with two people than one, especially when the one is a hopeless cook who usually forgets to even turn on the oven.

My head hurts.

I can't wait to get home.

Everything bores me. TV is boring. Reading is boring. Texting people is boring. Music is boring. And I *would* write, but I *can't*, because I have nothing to say that doesn't sound pathetic and petty and pointless.

No one really cares what a sixteen-year-old

thinks or feels, anyway.

I'm bored. Plain and simple.

Into the kitchen. Boil kettle for cup of tea in the hope that the caffeine will cure my headache without me having to resort to tablets with that taste that lingers in your mouth all day.

I take out a knife. It's sharp against my flesh. I only drag it lightly across my arm a couple of times, but it breaks the skin, leaving lines of blood.

I press a tissue against the cuts. They're not too bad. They'll be fine in a couple of weeks.

You told yourself you were going to stop doing it.

I know. But this is the last time. I promise.

Last time was also the last time, Abi.

Oh, get lost, inner child or conscience or whatever you are.

Outside, the sun begins to shine, the light flooding into the kitchen via the window.

Stupid me. It's getting hot outside and I'm stuck in long sleeves for the next week, at least. Stupid, stupid, stupid.

Chapter Twenty-One

It's two in the morning. I can't sleep, so, naturally, I am downstairs, on the computer.

C:\My Documents\Abi\Poems.doc

Now I know why all those poets went crazy or turned to alcohol. It's the words. You spend so much time looking for the right one, and then you look back over it a few days later, a few weeks later, and it's just not good enough. It doesn't work. It sounds stupid or pretentious or inappropriate. It's wrong. *You're* wrong.

I really should find a nice, non-frustrating occupation to throw myself into. Something that won't cause me to constantly doubt my ability at it.

Maybe I'm just one of those people who subconsciously puts themselves into situations where they'll feel miserable because it's safer than developing as a person and taking the risk of being happy.

Maybe I just like to write.

Maybe it's the same thing.

I trace a finger along the marks on my arm. Three thin lines. Not much. If you look closely, you can see faint dark pink lines criss-crossing underneath.

Why do you do it, you want to know.

Sometimes I really don't know. Sometimes I do it just because I *can*.

Chapter Twenty-Two

On Thursday we have a trip to a synagogue, in the hope that exposure to religions other than Catholicism will leave us enlightened and tolerant. It's really too bad that our religion teacher isn't coming along. She could use some enlightenment, seeing as she's about as tolerant as Hitler at the moment. ("Let's all be tolerant, girls, but only if people conform to what the Catholic Church wants.")

Karen is moaning about having to go. She knows it'll be boring.

"I think it'll be really interesting, actually," says Rebecca The Annoying Optimist. Rebecca, unsurprisingly, *loves* Transition Year, which seems to entitle her to lecture anyone who doesn't share her view. She doesn't seem to understand the idea of "agreeing to disagree". She thinks that she's the most rational, sensible person in the world, and that if she talks at you for long enough you'll come around to her way of thinking.

I'm not terribly enthusiastic about the afternoon tour, either. I suggest leaving at lunch-time to Karen. She's worried about getting caught. I have had ten minutes to think about it and have grown quite attached to the idea of not being here this afternoon.

Sarah, on the other hand, has physics in the afternoon.

"See you outside the gates," she tells me.

Fourth, Fifth and Sixth Years are allowed home for lunch, so there is nothing suspicious about walking out of the school grounds. We'll be marked

Stereotype

absent for the afternoon, but it will be assumed that we went home sick, or that a note was handed in, or something. It's easy to get away with missing an afternoon.

At the start of the year, caught up in the novelty of being able to go home for lunch, I used to do it every day. Then you get tired of it, and stop bothering.

We go to my house, since my parents won't be home until after five and Sarah's mother has been known to come home at lunch. (A fact that she learned last year when she and Fiona left early one day. It wasn't pretty.)

"So, how are you?" she asks, settling in for a Deeply Personal Conversation.

I shrug. "Fine."

"You always say that," she grins. "Seriously. Is everything OK?"

"Yeah," I say, and smile to show that I really, really mean it. And in a way I do. Everything *is* OK. What can I complain about, really? Nothing's *wrong*.

"How are things with you?" I ask.

"So-so," she admits.

"Just so-so? What's up?"

She shrugs. "It's stupid. And you don't want to hear about it."

"It's *not* stupid," I tell her firmly. "Come on. What is it?"

51

"Just this whole thing with Shane, and the band, and stuff . . ." she begins. "Are you sure you want to hear this? I know I've been going on about it a bit . . ."

"It's fine, go on."

"Well, it's great, in one way. I mean, I'm getting to know some really cool people, and I love the whole vibe. You know, the excitement that we're all really going to do this. But then there's the flipside of it all, where I wonder what the hell I'm doing there with all these incredibly talented and dedicated people. I mean, I've been looking at a lot of the stuff Shane writes. It's - amazing. He's seventeen. He's *seventeen* and he's writing stuff that most of the professionals out there wouldn't be able to write. You listen to him play it on the guitar and it's like he's - I don't know - ripped out your heart and turned it into music."

"He must be good, then," I say. Well, what else can I say?

Sarah rolls her eyes. "No shit, Sherlock."

I laugh.

She continues. "Anyway, it's depressing. I mean, what am I doing around someone like that?"

"If he didn't think you had talent, he wouldn't have bothered asking you if you were interested," I point out.

She doesn't look convinced. "I suppose . . . but

maybe he just feels sorry for me."

"He seems like the sort of person who takes music really seriously," I say.

She nods. "Oh, he is, yeah."

"So of course it makes *perfect* sense for him to surround himself with people who'll let him down and mess things up for him," I say pointedly.

She starts smiling. "OK, so maybe you're right."

"I'm always right," I kid.

"Oh, of course. How could I have forgotten? I am not worthy, oh great one."

"I forgive you, my child," I say solemnly.

"You're too kind."

"Yeah. I know." I grin.

Chapter Twenty-Three

"What are you doing home?" Greg asks suspiciously.

"We had a half day," I say in my 'well, *duh*' voice. It's useful when dealing with younger siblings.

"Oh." He pauses, then decides to continue the conversation. Wonderful. "I have *loads* of homework."

"You're in fourth class," I remind him.

"So?" he says defiantly. "We still get *loads* of

work to do."

"Sure. Whatever." I nod.

"You think you know everything," he snaps at me, storming out of the room.

"Someone could do with some therapy," Sarah notes.

"Me or him?" I smile.

"Oh, you're too far gone," she says. "Greg still has a chance of a normal life, but you? There's no hope."

"Hopeless, that's me."

"OK, what's up?"

"Nothing," I smile.

"Are you sure? You'd tell me if there was something wrong, right?" She sounds worried.

"Of course. Before I shoot myself, I'll call you," I tell her.

"That's all I wanted to know." She pauses. "Seriously, though, Abi, I worry about you."

"Yeah, I worry about me too," I say in an effort to keep the conversation light.

"You know what I mean." She tries to look annoyed, but can't quite pull it off. The Sarah-smile. Even when she's angry people can have a hard time figuring out whether she's serious or not. "I mean, you're *always* saying you're OK. And you're not."

"I'm fine," I say, wondering how many times I

can utter that phrase before it loses all meaning. Actually, I think I'm already past that point.

"No you're not. You're a teenager. It's practically mandatory to be at least a little crazy." She's half-joking, half-serious.

I shrug. "I'm crazy. I admit it."

"I think you're scared to let anyone get too close to you," she muses.

She is far too perceptive for her own good.

"Maybe," I say softly. "I just don't like talking about myself."

She puts on an exaggerated-sad face. "Not even to me?"

"Especially not to you, you nutcase," I grin.

"I always knew it!" she sighs theatrically.

And the serious talk is over. Cue a sigh of relief from me.

Chapter Twenty-Four

Let us resume the telling of Abi's Life Story, in non-chronological order. (Just to be different. As always.)

Flash back to sometime in Second Year, probably around this time two years ago. Angry Abi is sullen and alienated from her former friends. School has become a place of torment. (Wait, change the 'has become' to 'still is'.) Incidentally, her grades have never been higher. She doesn't know why. It's not as if she's throwing herself into her schoolwork. It's hard for her to find solace in anything.

It's more than just Leanne, more than just this school crap. It hurts to smile. Her mind will only entertain dark, morbid thoughts. Sometimes it feels like she's not there at all.

She is even slowly losing the enthusiasm to be angry.

She knows she can't go on like this forever. The thought of never being happy again scares her. She works hard on blocking out the darkness.

She is walking home one day and turns onto her road. She notices a thin, dark-haired girl sitting on the doorstep of one of the houses. They are in the same school, wearing identically hideous uniforms. Abi has seen her around school and sometimes walking home, recognising her vaguely. Their dads know each other, some community-related thing.

Now, let's be clear on this. Pretty people usually intimidate the hell out of me. But there was something different about her that made me call out, "You're locked out, huh?"

She smiled. "Yeah. Forgot my keys."

"If you want to call someone or anything, I have -"

"Nah, it's OK, I already called my mom," she

said, getting up and walking towards me. "She's not going to be home until later. She's still in work and then she has to go pick up my sister from music. You're Abigail, right?"

"Uh-huh. Abi."

"Sarah," she introduced herself. "You're in Second Year, yeah?"

"Yep."

"How's it going?"

"OK, I guess."

She grinned. "Second Year is hell. Of course, Third Year's worse. Just think, you've got *that* to look forward to next year."

"I can hardly wait," I laughed.

And we clicked, just like that. She ended up coming back to my house and waiting there until her mom got home.

"Hmmm. The Goo Goo Dolls. I approve," she said, picking up *Dizzy Up The Girl* from beside the CD player in the kitchen. "Now I know it's OK to hang out with you, seeing as you have good taste in music."

I smiled. "You're big into music, huh?"

"Only obsessively. I spend most of my money on CDs, write my own songs, that sort of thing."

"You write songs?" I was interested, and intrigued.

"Yeah. I know, I know. It's sad."

"No! I think it's cool. I mean, creating something - it's great. And it's fun."

She did her perceptive-stare thing for a moment. "Ah. We have an artist on our hands, I see. Not a composer . . . painter?"

I shook my head.

"A writer," she said firmly. "A poet, maybe?"

She was chancing it with the last part, but she was right. We did a little bit of creative-mind-bonding and then went to watch *The Simpsons*, thus sealing our friendship forever.

Chapter Twenty-Five

Thursday night. *Buffy. Angel.* Then sleep. Or at least an attempt.

My room is a bookworm's paradise. The first time Sarah saw my room she spent hours just looking through my bookcase.

I'm addicted to American young-adult novels. Short, sassy, and sophisticated - what I hide behind when I'm not up to reading grown-up type books. So I have a whole pile of them. *The Perks of Being A Wallflower. I Was A Teenage Fairy. Speak. Innocence. The Princess Diaries* (bought after much reluctance). *Keeping The Moon. Tiger Eyes. Among Friends. Sloppy Firsts.*

Stereotype

On the other hand we have the tome next to my bedside. (No, nor *War and Peace*. *The Journals of Sylvia Plath*, actually.) It's been sitting there for the past couple of weeks. Mostly I just look at the pictures, because it's hard to get into the actual journal part. I mean, it's not that it's boring - it's more like it's *intense*. Like when I read *The Bell Jar*. It took me two years to properly get into it. And then I read the rest of it within two days.

Her hair looks awful in most of the pictures, if you must know. I don't like those fifties hairstyles. But on the cover, she looks pretty. I think she was. Pretty, I mean. Her hair's down to her shoulders and wavy and she looks enigmatic - and young.

She was young, but you forget. You forget that her family and teachers knew she was talented in her teens, that she was published before her twentieth birthday. You forget that those amazing poems of hers were written in her twenties, as was The Bell Jar. And you forget that she never got to see her thirty-first birthday.

February 11, 1963. That's the date. You probably think I'm crazy for knowing it.

There's this picture of her and Ted - well, there are a couple of pictures of the two of them, but there's this one where he's got his arms around her, and they're both looking out into the distance, amazingly happy. It looks sort of posed, actually, but the joy is real.

Before college she writes about not wanting to die. Aged thirty she kills herself. Maybe she just wanted to take control of her own destiny instead of waiting around for fate to choose her death day. Maybe things were just that bad for her.

Maybe February 11 was the first day she ever thought about it and really meant it. Maybe she was planning it all her life, some little voice in the back of her head telling her that her life wasn't worth living.

(Read the journal, Abi, and quit boring us with your speculation. Yeah, yeah, I know.)

Chapter Twenty-Six

Thank God it's Friday. When I get into school Karen informs me that the synagogue was, as suspected, boring.

I smile. "I told you - you should've left."

"Did you go home on your own?" she asks.

"Nah, Sarah came with me," I say. See, Karen, I'm not necessarily going to be a loner just because you decide you'd prefer to stay in school to hang around with Leanne.

Call me bitchy, or obsessive, or whatever, but I like the fact that I'm closer to Sarah and even Fiona than Karen is. I guess Karen's lucky that she can fit in with any group, but I think the trouble with being universally liked is that it's harder to get to know people well.

Either that, or it's my way of trying to convince myself that it's better to have a few close friends than a crowd of semi-close ones, so I can feel better about my disastrous people skills.

Because it's the day before a bank-holiday weekend, the entertainment-related discussions have reached their peak. As have my stress levels. If one more person mentions St Patrick's Day, I'll scream.

This weekend I will *not* be going to the parade, or going out drinking, or anything remotely normal. I was planning to be completely reclusive. You have to admit there's something enchanting about the whole idea of cutting yourself off from the world to maximise your creative potential. You know, living alone, being all crazy and poetic . . . it *does* sound appealing.

But my plan to have a trial weekend of isolation has been thwarted. There's a party on Saturday night in Sarah's house. The infamous Shane will be there, as will the rest of the band. The final decision was made about the members yesterday. According to Sarah, one of Shane's friends desperately wanted to be involved. He's also desperately tone-deaf. I feel sorry for him.

So it's Sarah, Shane, and three of his friends, including, surprisingly enough, Caroline. I didn't know they were friends, but apparently they went to primary school together and live in the same estate.

I see Caroline on Friday afternoon. There's a hockey match on, one of the senior teams playing, and we're allowed to go out and watch it.

Since hockey doesn't terribly excite me, I end up talking to Caroline for the duration of the match.

"Hey! Are you going to the party?" she asks.

I nod. "Yeah, Sarah's making me."

She grins. "Good. It looks like there's going to a bunch of people from Shane's school there, and I don't know any of them. I was scared it was going to be just me and Sarah around, like, a hundred guys." She frowns. "Actually, maybe that wouldn't be that bad."

"You've always got Shane, anyway," I remind her.

"Ah, of course," she says. "Except I think he'll be too busy with Sarah on Saturday night."

"Does he like her?" I ask.

She shrugs. "I don't know. He says he just likes her as a friend, but -"

"But he acts like he does," I finish.

"Yeah."

OK, it's settled, he fancies her. I change the subject. "Have you guys decided on a name yet?"

Caroline frowns. "Shane came up with one, but we told him where to go with it."

I grin. "What was it?"

"God, I don't think I can even *pronounce* it right. Idio - idiosyncratic. I had to look it up when I went home."

"I like it," I muse.

"I bet you know what it means, too," she rolls her eyes.

"Sort of," I say. "Distinctive, unusual, individual."

She groans. "It took me ten minutes to find it in the dictionary and you know it off the top of your head. That's not scary at *all*. I didn't even know how to spell it."

"So probably not a good idea for a name, then," I say.

"Yeah. We all wanted something we actually understood, so we're still thinking of names."

Call me crazy, but that little story suddenly makes me interested in this Shane person. Big words impress me, OK? Of course, he probably picked it up from some pretentious rock song. But still . . .

I like the idea of us both knowing what a word meant while everyone else is confused, two misunderstood souls.

So, Saturday night, huh?

Chapter Twenty-Seven

Friday night is *Frasier* night. The whole family sits down to watch it, even Jess, who doesn't think it's "cool" to watch any programmes that your parents enjoy. (Not to mention your older sister. It's hard to believe Jess used to look up to me. Even up until she turned thirteen, just before Christmas, she used to borrow my clothes. Now she wouldn't be seen *dead* in anything *I'd* wear. Sigh. I should be devastated, but it's such a relief not to have to worry about her taking my stuff any more that I've forgotten to grieve.)

Is it just me or did all the fun go out of the Niles-and-Daphne relationship once they actually got together? I mean, the great thing about them was the hope that maybe one day they would get together, that Niles would finally confess his feelings for her. You wanted him to get her, and you felt sorry for the poor lovesick puppy. The excitement is in the "maybe". Once they actually became a couple? Blah. All the hope was gone.

Unrequited love is *much* more interesting. Even in real life. The possibility of something happening is what keeps you going.

Like me and Ronan. This was - oh, ages ago. First or Second Year, I suppose. He was a friend of Hannah's and I fell madly in love with him. Every spare moment of my time was devoted to dreaming about how we would profess our undying love for one another. Then Hannah said that she thought he liked me.

I should have been happy, delirious, over the moon. And I was - for about a day. It was wonderful being admired. It was a nice change. But the novelty wears off quickly, and you realise that the excitement has gone.

I stopped liking him. Then he stopped liking me, at which point I started liking him again. And so on. It went on for about three months, and the funny part is that nothing ever came of it. I never even kissed him.

In a way, the daydreams are more fun. Reality just can't compete.

Chapter Twenty-Eight

He writes a song for me, and sings it for me at the band's first public performance, gazing into my eyes intently. I stare up at him, loving him so much that it hurts.

Or maybe we're not together yet, and he sings it. I am in the audience, thinking, "Wow, what a great song" when he accidentally catches my eye, and looks embarrassed. It hits me - the song's about me. I look up at him, and he is both hopeful and scared. I smile, and he grins, throwing himself into the music.

Or maybe one of the other guys in the band starts to fancy me, and he thinks I'm interested, and gets jealous. One night he confronts me, somewhat awkwardly.

"I don't know what you're doing with him," he says.

"Why?" I ask, somewhat coquettishly. (I'm not at all sure if I can be coquettish, but it's a fantasy, so we're allowed take some liberties.)

"He just doesn't seem like your type."

"Really? So what is my 'type', then?"

"Someone - I don't know. Someone who appreciates you."

I look at him. It's one of those perceptive looks that Sarah's so good at.

He looks slightly embarrassed, but doesn't blush. "What?"

"Nothing," I say.

"You know . . . I really think you'd be better off without him."

"Why do you even care?" I ask, exasperated at this stage.

"Oh, for God's sake," he says, joining me in The Land of Frustration. "Why do you think I care, Abi?"

And then . . . he looks at me, and I look at him, and we kiss, and it's wonderful.

Or maybe I'm really drunk at the party, and can't even stand, and he has to carry me upstairs to Sarah's room. I'm practically unconscious at this stage, so he *watches me for a little while, and pushes strands of hair away from my face, his tender fingers lovingly running over my skin. (Fun to imagine; but if it actually happened the intimacy would be lost on me.)*

Or maybe we're alone in a room and we just talk. One of those wonderfully deep discussions where you realise how much you have in common. And he makes me laugh. And then I make him laugh. It's perfect.

Or maybe we're watching a movie and it's really emotional and he brushes a tear away from his eye. I look at him.

"What?" he says defensively.

"You're crying," I note in amusement.

He does the whole macho-man thing, denying all allegations of tears, before I tell him that I love sensitive guys.

"Especially cute ones," I add.

Or maybe I don't even *know* this guy. I've never met him, I don't know what he looks like, and the only thing I do know about him is that he's talented.

And has a wide vocabulary, which is why the daydreaming began. Aaagh! I ask you, how many sixteen-year-olds do *you* know who find big words a turn-on?

Chapter Twenty-Nine

On Saturday I am struck with a severe case of anti-social-itis. I don't want to go out. I don't want to see people. I just want to stay at home and read and watch TV and if that makes me a loser than so be it, because I'd prefer to be at home than out and not enjoying myself.

I consider making an excuse. "Look, Sarah, I'm feeling really sick. I don't think I can come tonight." Or plead a case of irrational parents. "My mom's really pissed off with me. She won't let me go." Or anything, any reason for not being able to go to a party full of people I don't know. People who take their music really seriously and can tell you everything you never wanted to know about a particular band or singer.

People who idolise Kurt Cobain and light a candle every April 5 and who can explain exactly why his death was such a tragedy and how he influenced the music of today, blah blah blah.

People who talk a lot about suicide and think it's cool. People who would sooner shoot themselves than listen to uplifting, pop music once in a while. People who are so pretentious that I would happily put them out of their misery and kill them.

I hate pretentiousness about *anything*. I hate people who only read "literature", like Jane in my class. Jane spent her childhood with her nose in the classics and thinks you're deprived if you haven't read *Pride and Prejudice* at least ten times. She uses English class to make comparisons between every male character ever created and Mr Darcy. Riveting, I assure you. (I mean, if you're going to take any literary character to use as a basis for comparison, it should really be Emily Brontë's Heathcliff. But that's beside the point.)

I wonder if Sarah will even care if I don't go. If I'm not there it'll give her a chance to spend more time with her instantly-acquired music-related friends, and before I know it, we'll be drifting apart. I'll call to her house one day before school only to be told that she's already left. I'll suggest doing something for the weekend and find that she has other plans that I was never told about. I'll ring her on the phone and she'll find some excuse to hang up after five awkward minutes.

I'll go back to being Lonely Abi. And even though I enjoy being alone a lot of the time, it's much worse to have it thrust upon you because no one wants to be around you.

I really don't want that to happen. Besides, I usually have a good time once I actually go out. And I have the rest of the weekend to be my usual anti-social self.

So . . . what am I going to wear?

Chapter Thirty

I run into Graham's mother while I'm walking down to Sarah's. Mrs - sorry, "Anna, call me Anna" - O'Brien. Considering there's all of ten metres between my house and Sarah's, it's surprising I see her at all.

I happen to like Anna, despite the intensely obnoxious nature of her son. She, after all, has no idea what an asshole she's raised, and I think she always secretly hoped that I'd become Graham's girlfriend and eventually wife and mother of her grandchildren, and so on.

We do the hi-how-are-you exchange, followed by a don't-you-look-lovely-where-are-you-off-to on her part, followed by an explanation from me, followed by an oh-enjoy-yourself.

She says goodbye and walks off, weighed down with green bags from Superquinn. I think about her going home and telling Graham that she was talking to me.

I imagine Graham filling her up with lies about what a horrible person I am. Funny that I care more about what his mom thinks of me than what he does. Then again, I have a tendency to seek approval from authority figures and/or role models. It's part of my insecurity complex.

I try to present myself as a quiet-but-polite girl to

adults, an intelligent and reasonable teenager. This obviously excludes my parents and anyone who actually knows me well, because fooling them would be impossible. Not that my parents know me that well, but still.

I wonder what Anna would think of me if she saw the scars on my arm. Recent, still red, still painful. Considering it makes me feel uneasy. I don't want anyone to find out what a mess I am, I realise slowly in something akin to an epiphany.

Obviously I am nowhere near as messed up as the kids who have *real* problems. You know what? I hate that term. "Real" problems. Who defines what's real and what's not? It's a real problem if it involves death, abuse or illness, but not real if it involves anything else? Real if you've got a prescription for Prozac, not real if you just don't want to go out to a party? You're only allowed to complain if you have a real problem, but if it's just melodramatic teen angst, forget about it. It's not important. You are irrelevant.

I am irrelevant and I hate it. Surprise, surprise.

Chapter Thirty-One

I find myself thinking of that debate in Irish during the party. The one about the uniforms. One advantage that we never mentioned was their ability to hide just how skinny some people are so that the not-so-skinny people can feel a little better.

I'm also reminded of why I hate colour days. Well, in a way I love getting to wear my own clothes into school, but in another way I hate the fact that all the thin people wear clothes to emphasise that and I'm left feeling rather elephant-like.

And it's ridiculous because on a good day I know that I've got a relatively good figure. Maybe not wonderful, but it's not that bad.

I just hate the way that everyone else seems to be prettier, thinner, better than me. I don't want to compete with anyone. It's pointless.

Everyone else has make-up plastered on, too. Well, the girls do. The guys - for the most part - don't. I'm wearing a little eye shadow and tinted lip-balm. I feel severely inferior.

I think most of the girls here are from school, although I'm not sure. I don't know that many of the Fifth Years. It's not like Sarah has parties regularly. Or ever. Not like this. Not with the loud music and people spilling out into the back garden. Sarah's sister is upstairs, locked away in her room. Their parents are away for the weekend and she's supposed to be in charge and not let any wild parties be thrown. Because she's the desperately "good" type - sort of like Rebecca The Annoying Optimist - they know they can trust her to keep things under control.

Which is why she's made Sarah promise to clean up thoroughly tomorrow morning. Fiona and I are staying over to help, on the condition that anyone throwing up is her responsibility.

Fiona, I notice, is doing a wonderful job of mingling. I am the wallflower, watching - and utterly bored. I don't know most of these people. I hate parties. Why am I here?

I could just hide out in Sarah's room until everyone leaves. Read a book, watch TV, escape from *this*.

I hate drunk people. I think I inherited this from my non-alcohol-drinking parents, who are always the designated drivers at an event, the sober people who end up taking care of the ones who can barely walk. Now I know how they feel, surrounded by incoherent idiots.

The party has barely begun, so not everyone has reached that stage just yet, but a lot of people were drinking before they arrived. That annoys me too. I mean, what's the point? (Oh, God, I'm turning into my parents. Help!)

I go into the kitchen to get another glass of water, debating whether or not to follow the "if you can't beat 'em, join 'em" rule and go for a Smirnoff Ice instead.

Sarah is sitting on the table with someone who I presume to be Shane. He looks vaguely familiar, and I can remember watching *American Pie* with him and Sarah at her house.

"Abi! Having fun?" she asks.

I shrug. "Yeah, I suppose so."

"Hey, Abi," Shane says.

"Hi," I smile. Behold, ladies and gentlemen, my amazing conversational skills!

Awkward silence. To have something to do, I get my drink. (I choose to "join 'em" and take a bottle of Smirnoff Ice. Total rebel, that's me.)

"So, this is awkward," grins Sarah.

Shane and I laugh. Then silence again.

"That was meant to break the ice," Sarah says pointedly.

"Oh! Have you guys come up with a name for the band yet?" I ask.

"Still throwing around ideas," says Shane.

"No, *you're* throwing around big words," Sarah tells him.

He shrugs, grinning.

I look at him. He's not in typical rocker attire. Just jeans, and a semi-loose but not excessively baggy plain black T-shirt. I'm somewhat impressed by the non-statement he's making.

He also happens to be quite attractive, if you were wondering.

74

Stereotype

Chapter Thirty-Two

Shane, Sarah and I do the small-talk thing for a couple of minutes; then he leaves to go and talk to his friends.

She watches him, fondly, as he walks away. "He's great, isn't he?"

"Yeah." He's got a fantastic smile, anyway. How much can you tell about a person from the minimal amount of interaction we've had? I know that he's into music, and I know that he laughed at *American Pie*. In other words, nothing that distinguishes him from everyone else of his age and gender.

I wonder what he'd think if he saw my scars, and whether he's the sheltered "why would you do that?" type or the hardened "yeah, so what?" type.

And it doesn't matter, anyway, because that's not me. That's not who I am. I'm never going to do it ever again, because I don't *want* to be the poor-little-attention-seeking girl. People like that sicken me. I hate them.

I am just going to be normal. Well, not *normal* normal. I mean, my motto is like that Avril Lavigne song. I want to be "Anything But Ordinary". I don't want to be normal, but a touch of normality couldn't hurt. I could live with being creative and wacky. I would *love* to be thought of as creative and wacky.

Instead of, you know, weird, freaky and definitely abnormal. Not to mention ugly. Looks compensate for so much in this world. Take Ciara in my class. She's quiet and mousy and has been getting up to all kinds of crazy things this year, like doing her homework and handing in projects on time. But she's pretty and skinny and looks *right*, so she fits in with Hannah and Leanne and Tina and everyone.

I *ache* to be thought of as pretty. It's blatantly unfair that people like Tina get to be attractive and slim when they do nothing but complain about how hideous they are and spend half their lives in the gym trying to perfect their figure.

And yeah, I know what you're thinking. "But Abi, maybe it's just that everyone hates the way they look, and I'm sure they think that you're pretty."

The world would be a wonderful place if it actually worked that way, but it doesn't. Welcome to reality. Some people are attractive. Some are not. I fall into the second category.

I do, however, know when to use *you're* and *your* in essays, something which a significant percentage of my class still haven't mastered.

(Sorry. Feeling inferior makes me bitchy.)

Sarah, still perched on the table, looks depressingly great. She's gone for a semi-gothic look tonight, in black and red velvet and lace. She has the *perfect* figure. You know the way that if you look hard enough at someone, you can find some flaw? Or maybe not even a flaw to you, but something that you know *they* hate. Like Fiona thinks that her thighs are too big. (They're not.) Sarah is perfectly proportioned, with curves in all the right places. Fiona and I told her that once.

"But what's the point of having a good figure when you have a face like *this*?" she moaned. You'd swear she was the Bride of Frankenstein or something. In fairness, though, she never complains that much about how she looks. None of us does. It should be one of those things that doesn't matter between friends. *Should* be.

I am still sipping at my Smirnoff Ice, perhaps in the hope that if I drink enough of it, I'll be able to look in the mirror and think I look attractive.

"You want me to introduce to you to people?" Sarah asks.

I think about it. "No."

She laughs. "Not in the party mood?"

"Not really."

"Oh, well. Stay in here for a while and talk to me."

"You should be out there mingling. You're the hostess," I smile.

She rolls her eyes. "They're getting along fine

without me. There's music, there's drink, that's all they need."

Our lives are veering dangerously close towards the land of teenage normality. I wonder if she realises this, and has opted to stay on the path anyway.

Chapter Thirty-Three

We end up being social and friendly after all. Shane drags us out of the kitchen and in to talk to some of his friends. The conversation turns to football, and I watch, mildly amused, as the guys, and a couple of avid female fans, get all worked up about it. Caroline and I exchange we-could-be-here-for-a-while looks.

It's not as bad as I thought it would be. For the most part, the guys are moderately intelligent, and some are even speaking in whole sentences as opposed to grunts at regular intervals. I'm impressed.

I find myself discussing all things musical with Hugh, one of the band members. He's a U2 fanatic, so we debate which of their albums is the best, the three main contenders being *The Joshua Tree*, *Achtung Baby* and *All That You Can't Leave Behind*.

Hugh, being a drummer, is talking about Larry

Mullen when Shane joins in. "Yeah, but come on now, they'd be nothing without Bono."

Hugh seems to have heard this before, many times. "Shane wants to *be* Bono," he tells me conspiratorially.

I grin. "How sweet," I tell Shane. "We all need a hero."

"So who's yours?" he asks, deflecting the attention from his own hero-worship.

I shrug. I really have no idea. I mean, I love Sylvia Plath and all that, but I certainly have no intention of dying at thirty.

"Lisa Simpson," I finally say, half-joking.

He grins. "Not Homer?"

"I'm not the Homer type."

"No, I suppose you're not."

What's that supposed to mean? I want to ask, but don't.

The first thing Sarah asks me, once everyone's gone, is what I thought of Shane.

"He's nice!" I say for what feels like the millionth time.

"*Nice*? That could be anyone."

It's almost two in the morning. My vocabulary isn't the best at this time of the day. "He's interesting," I add. And yeah, I suppose I'm telling the truth. But he's a tad on the intimidating side and he can make me feel uncomfortable and I'm not exactly sure what I think of him, or what he thinks of me.

"What did *you* think?" she asks Fiona.

"The same," Fiona yawns. "Look, Sarah, would you just admit that you fancy him and stop interrogating us!"

"I don't," she protests.

"Sure, sure," Fiona and I say.

"Besides -" she begins, and we all know that whenever anyone starts talking like that, it clearly means that they're interested in someone, but are trying desperately to prove otherwise. "*Besides*, even if I *did*, he's not interested in me."

"How do you know?" Fiona demands. "Have you asked him?"

"I just *know*," Sarah insists. "I think he likes Abi."

"*What*?" I splutter. She's clearly delusional.

"Well, he was talking to you all night," she says.

"Yeah, me *and* Hugh *and* Caroline and anyone else that wanted to join in. You're reading too much into this," I tell her. "Besides, Caroline thinks he likes you."

"Well, he doesn't," she says firmly.

Fiona is watching us with amusement. "Are you two going to fight over him?"

"Don't be stupid," I say.

"I don't even like him," Sarah says, but the lack of conviction in her voice is obvious.

"Sarah, he likes you," I tell her.

"No, he doesn't," she says. Yes, it's true, denial isn't just a river in Egypt. I know *exactly* why she's doing this. If he doesn't like her, then she can convince herself that there's no point in flirting with him or asking him out, because it's pointless. It lets her off the hook. I do it all the time.

Besides, there's no way he likes me. I mean, normal, nice, sane guys never like me. Generally even the crazy ones avoid me. But it's OK, because I don't like him either.

Chapter Thirty-Four

"So, do you like Shane?" Fiona whispers to me the following morning. Well, mid-afternoon. Time to clean up. The fun is only just beginning . . .

I have one of those pounding headaches where you can actually *hear* the veins throbbing. I'm not in the mood to discuss Shane. "No," I say curtly.

"*OK*," Fiona says huffily.

Great. Just great. Exactly what I need, one of my friends being pissed off with me. Well, I knew I couldn't hide my bitchiness forever. It had to emerge someday, and then they'd see me for what I really am and hate me.

Last night Shane and I were discussing the band.

"I want us to be really original, you know?" he said earnestly.

"It's hard to be original," I said, thinking *And I don't think you're going to achieve that goal. For all your talk you're still just a seventeen-year-old who thinks he can change the world with his music.*

And the truth is that although a lot of musicians think they can change the world with music, no one has ever succeeded. Sarah disagrees with me, citing John Lennon as an example. Great musician, sure, but there are still wars going on. There are famines, there are diseases that we can't cure. And I'm not one of those deeply-concerned political-activist types, but even I know that there are still so many problems in the world and music isn't the answer. Or films, or books, or whatever art form you choose.

Yeah, I'm a cynic. A poetic cynic, how about that?

Of course, we ended up talking about whether art could change the world or not. In response to my it's-hard-to-be-original statement he said, "Yeah, it's hard, but not impossible. You just have to be honest, and then anything's possible" which naturally led to a heated debate.

"You don't really believe that," he said, smiling. "You just want to be different and argue with me."

"No, I just think that you're a little naïve, that's all," I replied.

"And I think you're a little too caught up in the idea of thinking that you're better than everyone else to accept the fact that you secretly agree with me."

I had no answer to that. Mostly because he was a little bit - not completely, mind you - right. And even though it was all in good fun, and we kept being friendly for the rest of the night, I was mildly annoyed with him.

Caroline and Hugh were coming back from the kitchen with drinks, and rather than involve them in the discussion, I finished it with a simple, very mature gesture.

I stuck my tongue out at him.

It elicited a grin. I hated him for being patronising, and loved him for the way he smiled.

Chapter Thirty-Five

"I think we're finished," Sarah declares.

I don't think she's ever going to have a party again. She was cleaning up the bathroom. Let's just say that although it was great that anyone who was sick managed to get in there in time, some people have trouble with their aim.

"I'm going to go home and *sleep*," Fiona says, yawning. She hugs us both and leaves. She doesn't seem annoyed with me any more, which is a relief. We're both just in bad moods today, she because she hasn't slept, me because of that excruciating headache.

"You going, too?" Sarah asks.

"Yeah, I'd better," I say. I don't have to go. I could stay, chat, whatever. But I want to leave. The painkillers at home are calling out to me.

I want to talk to her about Shane, but I'm not sure how to bring it up. And I'm pretty sure she's still working on fooling herself into thinking she doesn't have a chance.

"See ya," she smiles.

I arrive home to jokes about wild parties, hangovers and strippers. My parents either still truly believe that at sixteen, I am innocent and my friends are equally demure, or they're living in Denial-Land. I debate telling them about the friend of Shane's who danced around in his underwear towards the latter half of the night, but decide they're better off not knowing.

Besides, it's not like I go out all the time. And unlike some people I can think of, I'm always able to walk in a straight line at the end of the night.

So was Shane, last night, but that's beside the

point. It doesn't make him a good person.

I don't know why I'm even thinking about him. I mean, he is the epitome of everything that I don't like about my generation. Pseudo-intellectual, pretentious, idealistic, "unique".

And I do *not* think that I'm better than everyone else. I'm just . . . not like them, that's all.

And maybe he isn't, either. Maybe none of us is, maybe we all really are individuals, but then I think about Rebecca The Annoying Optimist, the Bleach Brigade, the Pretty People, the It's-Cool-To-Be-Depressed Crowd, and it's just too hard to believe that any of them have anything truly original to say.

Chapter Thirty-Six

The thing I hate about *The Catcher In The Rye* and the book that's been referred to as its twenty-first century equivalent, *The Perks Of Being A Wallflower*, is that you *understand* why the narrators are so messed up. You know what I mean. They have reasons. There's a traumatic past, involving the death of a loved one and abuse as a child, and they've been to psychiatrists.

I wonder if it's just that Americans have this talk-it-all-out attitude, and that's why they love sending kids off to therapists. They're big into finding quick cures for problems. If therapy doesn't work it's off to the GP for your Prozac prescription. In Ireland it's a different view - work *through* your problems, there are always people worse off than you, life is hard, everyone goes through tough times.

Maybe it's just me who thinks that. Maybe it's just me saying these things because I would love the thought of being *declared* a troubled child. Diagnosed. And then fixed.

"Made tidy," like in that U A Fanthorpe poem, 'Patients'. I like it because I think maybe she knows what I mean, she understands this feeling that no one else seems to have. Or maybe she doesn't and I'm only seeing what I want to.

Of course, if they told me I was crazy then I'd hate it. I'm the ultimate tantrum-throwing toddler, wanting everything that I don't have.

Chapter Thirty-Seven

On Monday we all head off to Mass together. The whole family. St Patrick's Day is one of the three occasions, along with Christmas and Easter, when we all have to go. The rest of the time we don't. I mean, my parents do, every single Sunday, but then

Jess and I started refusing to go, and Greg decided to be oh-so-original and join in. Eventually they gave up on the three of us - although they still have some hope for converting Greg back to Catholicism. Maybe it's not too late for him, they think.

I think it's their way of being tolerant while secretly hoping that it's just a phase (*everything's 'just a phase'*) and we'll grow out of it.

Jess is extremely anti-religious, thinks all priests are child-molesters, thinks all religions are cults, et cetera. I'm not. I just can't believe in any of it. I would support almost everything the Catholic church has to say if it wasn't for the deity element of it.

I used to pray every night, the same way that someone with OCD has to wash their hands seventeen times or flip a light switch on and off. *Dear God, please don't let anything bad happen to my family and friends and please don't let any of them go blind or die, amen.*

I was such a worrier as a child. I was haunted by nightmares of my parents dying. Every time they were out late I panicked. I stopped praying and for a while I just blocked everything out. No more worrying about anything serious, just reassure yourself that's everything *will* be OK.

It's like I can only concentrate on either the serious or the trivial. And the serious stuff feels worse, but the trivial things make me do stupid things like cut myself or scream at someone. I don't get it. I really don't.

Chapter Thirty-Eight

Another Tuesday has arrived too quickly. Once more I have forgotten my tracksuit for Irish dancing. You'd almost think that I was doing this deliberately. Caroline seems to be playing the part of an involved, enthusiastic student and taking part in the dancing this week, so I'm on my own. Well, not technically on my own, but it feels that way. There are a couple of Earnest Students and a few of the Bleach Brigade in the same boat as I am, but for all intents and purposes, I'm alone.

Some people can't stand not being surrounded by people to talk to. I'm not like that. I sit quietly at the back of the supervision room and stare at my homework journal. The cover is too crowded to even attempt to fit in another squiggle.

Sometimes I wish Transition Year would just finish. Everyone's always saying about how much they're dreading Fifth Year and how hard it's going to be after this, but I'm so sick of doing nothing. I just want to get *out* of here.

The work is not going to be a problem. Well, it is. I mean, it's hard. But it's the spaces in between the work that's the problem, the hanging-out-with-people-in-your-class part.

They don't really care if I'm there or not. Karen might, yeah, but she's generally too busy trying so hard to be popular, or whatever it is she's trying to do, to notice. I'm not a part of their little group. I hover on the outskirts, slipping away to talk to Sarah half the time. For them, school is a time to be with their friends. For me, it's . . . just school. Just a place that I have to be for another couple of years, and then I'll leave and never look back.

It makes me feel kind of sad in a way, though. I remember in First Year we were told that we'd look back fondly on this time in our lives, and that we'd make lifelong friends in school. And yes, it was sentimental bullshit that had half the year rolling their eyes, but I always get inspired by things like that. I'm pathetic, I know. It just makes me feel like I'm missing out on the whole teenage experience. Everyone else is busy making lifelong friends and going out and having fun and enjoying their youth - and I'm sitting at home in front of the TV, or the computer, or listening to CDs.

Don't get me wrong - I *love* doing all of that. But sometimes I wonder whether I'll look back on my teenage years and regret not . . . participating.

Hi, I'm Abigail the Wallflower, welcome to my life.

Chapter Thirty-Nine

Breaktime is actually OK. I talk to Hannah for most of it. We used to be such good friends. I guess she feels sorry for me or something. I used to completely idolise her. She always seemed so individualistic.

"Seemed" being the key word, of course. I was young and naïve and didn't realise that it was, for the most part, an act.

In fairness to her, though, she's an interesting and thoughtful person. If it wasn't for the fact that she's so close to the others, we might still be friends.

And, you know, if I wasn't such a total freak. But I digress.

During Religion class we discuss the sanctity of life and why abortions are evil.

"Don't you think women should have the option of having an abortion?" I have to ask.

Narrowed eyes. "I think women should take responsibility for their actions. When you become sexually active" (cue a snort of laughter from the back of the class) "you have to realise that you have to accept the consequences."

I refuse to let it go. "So you think that one mistake should determine the rest of someone's life? Shouldn't women be able to choose whether *they* want to bring a child into the world or not?"

"If they're pregnant, then they've already made that decision," she responds, sounding like she wants this debate to end and go back to reading out what's on the handouts.

"So you think that sex serves no other purpose apart from procreation?" I demand.

More laughs. A couple of smirks from semi-relevant people like Hannah. The teacher decides to change the subject. I hate her.

The thing is that I'm only pro-choice because I'd prefer to be liberal than super-conservative, sanctimoniously preaching about how life is a gift from God. If I got pregnant accidentally - although the chances of that happening are slim to none, since I hear that sex is necessary for that to happen - I wouldn't even consider abortion. Or adoption. I'd want to have the baby. I just like the idea of people being able to choose what they want to do.

Then, of course, people will complain about others having the right to do what they want, because they disagree with it, and there's a fine line between the right to choose and completely anarchy. Which is why I could never go into politics. It just seems too complicated and confusing and frustrating, and I'd just want to hand out cups of tea and tell people to calm down and stop getting so worked up over being *right*.

But isn't that what I want? To be right all the time? To think that I'm the one who knows best?

Chapter Forty

I run into Sarah and Fiona on my way to their classroom. "Heya," Fiona says. "We're going to the shop. You coming?"

"Sure," I shrug.

"Yeah, come to the shop with the girl who has delusions of grandeur," mutters Sarah.

"What did I miss?" I ask.

"Wendy, being full of herself," Sarah responds.

"She decided to come over and have a friendly chat with Sarah today," Fiona explains. "She was all, 'Oooh, you're in a band, that's so *cute*'. Completely condescending, you know? She went on like that for about five minutes, being so *fake*, and when Sarah finally told her to get lost, she turned into a bitch. She was *looking* for an excuse to pick a fight."

I don't even know who Wendy is, but I have a feeling I know the type. There's about twenty of them in my year. At least.

"Why would she *bother*?" I wonder.

"Because she's a desperately sad person who needs to make other people feel bad so she can feel better about herself," Fiona responds.

"And she likes Shane," Sarah speaks up.

"That too," Fiona says smoothly.

I grin.

"It just *kills* her that someone who isn't *popular* and *cool* is spending time with her new obsession," Sarah says. "She doesn't even *know* him, you know? She just found out that he's a guitar player and thinks that it'd be cool to go out with him. She's so completely fake, it's unbelievable."

"Does he know her?" I ask.

"No, but Hugh does. She lives near him and she's always trying to get him to introduce her to Shane. He thinks she's a bitch, too, by the way."

"Good judge of character," Fiona comments.

"So, she thinks you're going to end up going out with Shane?" I ask Sarah.

"Yeah, I know, it's ridiculous," she says.

"That's not what I meant," I say.

"I know," she grins. "Listen - apparently Shane fancies someone in our school."

"How'd you find that out?" I ask. "How many people *know* him, anyway?"

She shrugs. "Not that many, it's not like he's a - I don't know, *rugby player* or something."

Fiona and I smile. Sarah has nothing but contempt for rugby players.

"But Wendy's crowd know who he is because

she's madly in love with him, so when they heard that -"

"They assumed that he fancied her?" I guess.

"Well, of course, yes," Fiona says. "Because she's so his type, you know?"

"But it gets better," Sarah says gleefully. Funny how gossiping about someone who's been obnoxious to you cheers you up, I think. "Apparently - and I think it's all a load of crap in the first place, by the way - but *apparently* this is someone who was at the party on Saturday. Because he was talking to her then."

It could be me, it could be me. Maybe it's just a silly rumour but oh, *oh*, it could be me.

"And she thinks it's you?" I ask.

"Yep. Because she knows someone who was there, who said he saw Shane talking to me. And being the complete *idiot* that she is, she assumes that I must be the only girl that he was talking to. Which is why she's decided to be completely obnoxious towards me." She sighs, back in depressed mode. "Wait, there was something good about this story. What was it?"

"Abi," Fiona says.

"What?" I say, just as Sarah goes, "Oh, of *course*."

"Of course what?" I ask.

"Well, if it's true . . . I mean, you spent the entire night talking to Shane."

"Not - the *entire* night," I say.

She laughs. "Come on, Abi. I know you like him."

"I don't!" I protest.

Fiona rolls her eyes. "Where have I heard this before?"

"You do," Sarah says.

"What about you?" I ask.

"What about me?" she says innocently.

"You like him."

She shrugs it off. "Maybe, maybe not. It doesn't matter. I'm not the one he likes."

"You might be," I point out.

"Look, we don't even know if what Wendy thinks is true or not," Fiona points out. "Knowing her, it's complete crap. So how about we just forget about Shane and have a nice, *peaceful* lunch-time?"

And it starts to rain.

Chapter Forty-One

After purchasing a considerable quantity of chocolate, we go back to school, somewhat reluctantly. There's nowhere to go when it rains, apart from someone's house, and we're all too lazy to make that much effort.

"Want to go and talk to Caroline?" Sarah asks

when we get back, obviously not wanting to return to her own classroom.

"Sure, OK," I shrug.

We actually run into Caroline as she's coming out the door, and end up sitting out in the corridor, legs stretched out while First Years trotting towards the tuck shop step tentatively over them.

Sarah fills in her in the Wendy situation before asking, "Shane didn't happen to mention to you whether he likes anyone, did he?" She tries to be casual about it but it comes off as very, very obvious that she really wants to know.

Caroline shakes her head. "I haven't been talking to him since the party. But I get the impression he likes you."

"Oh," Sarah says. Tries not to smile. Fails.

"You like him," Caroline declares with a grin.

"Maybe a little," she admits.

I bite my nails.

Of course it couldn't have been me.

It shouldn't matter. I barely know him.

I should be happy for Sarah.

I shouldn't feel like this. I have no right to feel this *bad*.

I should be used to it by now. Knowing that it's impossible for anyone to actually be interested in me. It's never going to happen. While my friends participate in the teenage-romance experience, I'm sitting on the sidelines. Ugly. Unwanted. Alone.

And it's not fair. It's not fair that I have to be like this, that I can't be pretty and thin and interesting and talented and confident and lovable. It's not fair that Sarah gets to be all of those things.

And *why* don't I bring razor-blades into school?

Chapter Forty-Two

Careers again. I think: future. I think: escape.

I think about being a crazy reclusive writer, à la Emily Dickinson. Spend the rest of my days hiding from the world, living behind a legacy of beautiful poems. Preferably not as morbid as her, though. Fewer funerals in brains; more fluffy bunnies and odes to chocolate.

With maybe a couple of angst-ridden, depressing rants thrown in for good measure, because we all know that I'm not exactly Little Miss Sunshine.

Ciara is asking about law, veterinary medicine, physiotherapy. All those courses that are designed for over-achievers, requiring so many points that it makes your head hurt just thinking about how many A's you'd need.

Already you can see the different attitudes towards the Leaving developing. There are the over-achievers, who are determined to put in the work and get the points for what they want. There are the under-achievers, who have decided that they're not going to do that well, and that's that; they can't do the course they want. There are the indifferents, who figure that it doesn't mean anything anyway. There are the unrealistics, the ones who want to do the same courses as the over-achievers and think that somehow the points will miraculously appear. There are the in-denials, who are refusing to think about their future.

I'm semi-ambitious. I want an A in English. Just because. And then I want enough points to get into Arts. That's it.

Two years, three months, and it'll be over. I can leave. I can get away from everyone.

And find people exactly like that at college.

Depressing thought. Going through life and having it all be just a repeat of your schooldays.

It gets better, right?

The bell goes. "Abi, are you walking?" Karen asks.

"Yeah," I say, unable to help adding, "like I usually do."

"Wait for me, will you?"

"Sure," I shrug.

Karen usually gets a lift. And when she doesn't, she and Hannah hang around and smoke before going home. She only walks home with us when we have something planned for the evening.

It's probably an attempt at making sure she doesn't fall out of the me/Sarah/Fiona group, just in case Leanne decides to stop being friends with her. After refusing to come to Sarah's party because she was going into town with *them*, I mean.

You were wondering why she wasn't there, huh? Too busy with her real friends, I suppose. Sarah was all, "Oh, sure, that's fine" since her party was an impromptu thing anyway. I happen to know that they'd only arranged to go into town that day, and that she could have easily gotten out of it. Most of them weren't sure whether they could go or not. But I guess she made her choice.

I'm not really bitter about it or anything. I just don't like being the second choice, the runner-up, the back-up friend.

But I guess maybe I've been treating her like that as well sometimes. Staying friends with her so that I won't be such a total outcast in our class.

It's primary school all over again.

"Heya," Sarah greets us both when we leave the classroom.

"Hey," Karen says. "How was the party?"

"It was . . . good," she shrugs. Smiles.

"How's what's-his-face? The one you're pretending not to fancy?"

"Shane?" she laughs. "He's fine." Another laugh. "He's *really* fine."

Karen grins. "I see. Anything happen between the two of you?"

"Not yet," she says, "but - give it time!"

She's gone from denying it, to half-admitting she likes him, to completely infatuated and delighted at the thought that he likes her. Meanwhile I've gone from not sure that I like him, to insane jealousy at the thought of him liking Sarah, to planning out my life as a reclusive poetry-writing spinster. Which one of us got the better deal here?

Chapter Forty-Three

I am not going to hurt myself. I am not going to hurt myself. I am - oh, why do I care? I *want* to, OK? So I'm going to do it.

There. Did it.

And I'm screwed-up girl again. Start taking me seriously, stop thinking it's just part of growing up, *listen* to me! I hurt and I *hurt* and I don't know why because there is no why, there's just me with all these emotions that I don't understand, me being angry and upset and silent, me wanting attention but not being able to trust anyone enough to let them see the real me, me sitting on my bed with a clump of tissues pressed against my bleeding arm and feeling like I need to cry but not being able to.

And instead of telling someone about this, I'm just going to sit here and be miserable and feel sorry for myself, because that's what I do so well.

I want to scream.

But I can't do that. The neighbours might complain. People would think I'm crazy. What's crazy is that more people don't go around screaming every so often. It'd solve a lot of problems. Scream and you feel better afterwards. But that wouldn't be normal, now would it? So instead people find some other way to deal with a surge of emotion, and they punch a pillow or squeeze an ice cube, or more likely they smash windows or yell at someone or start a fight or pour themselves a drink or light up a joint or pull out their hair.

And if it's public enough, or if you're found out, they do something with you, they send you to jail or therapy or rehab. Then, if you're lucky, you can emerge with a clean slate. You get a second chance, and it seems like you've recovered.

But *you're* not the problem. You're not the one who couldn't scream because people might think you were crazy.

Chapter Forty-Four

It's so funny to listen to Jess talk to her friends. None of them has a remotely intelligent thought in their heads, the accents are as rough as they come, the amount of curse words per sentence shoots up drastically. All of them trying to be experts on the music industry, as dismissive as possible of everything they consider pop, all trying to impress each other.

I guess that's what it's like being thirteen, always trying to prove that you're cool enough for the group that you want to hang out with. Conformity in the extreme.

I was never *that* bad, was I? I mean, I know I was pretty bad. Desperately wanting to be cool, acting differently around certain friends, avoiding the undesirable unpopular people even if I wanted to be friends with them and felt bad about shunning them. But I was always a little individualistic. Or weird. Whichever word you'd prefer to use.

She's worse than I was, right? Or maybe it's just that she's succeeded in conforming, whereas I never could.

But they all think that they're being different. They're rebelling against society, blah blah blah. They seem to be under the impression that teenagers being rebellious and unwilling to respect authority is a new idea.

How sweet.

Yes, I'm being condescending. What's the point of being so fixed in your views that you automatically think that anything the older generation says is worthless? You have to pick your fights instead of arguing just for the sake of it.

Generally speaking, of course.

Chapter Forty-Five

Wednesday afternoon. Cooking. Caroline and I are making some kind of spicy stir-fry thing. She keeps sneaking in extra ingredients, usually for the purpose of making the dish even spicier than it is. I think we should bring it to the staffroom and offer it round to the teachers. Might be interesting to watch them spontaneously combust. Evacuate the (rare) nice teachers beforehand, though. The ones who treat you like actual human beings. I think we have about three in the entire school, which is probably above the national average. We should feel so privileged.

And in fairness, very few of the staff are actively evil.

My right sleeve is pushed up past my elbow; my

left sleeve is only pushed up a little. Must hide those nasty marks, after all.

If she saw them - what would she say? Would I make an excuse, or would I smile enigmatically and say "What do you *think* happened?" in a semi-regretful tone. You know, a we-all-have-problems-this-is-my-way-of-dealing-what-can-you-do? sort of voice. Act like it's not a big deal, while she worries and realises that you are in fact a Troubled Adolescent.

Maybe she'd even go to a teacher and tell them. Or the guidance counsellor. That'd be interesting, actually. Then there'd be a big confrontation scene. Well, not big. But dramatic. Quietly dramatic.

"Abigail, I want to talk to you." Serious face.

I smile. "Sure, what is it?" Helpful-student face.

Teacher finds it hard to believe that this lovely girl could have hurt herself.

"I've been talking to another student, who was concerned about you. She thinks you're cutting yourself."

I say nothing. This is my admission.

Or maybe I say something. I am, after all, in helpful-student mode, acting as positive and upbeat as Rebecca The Annoying Optimist.

Yes, I think I'll speak.

"What? Who told you that?" I ask, looking innocent and confused.

"Abigail, I'm going to have to ask you to show me

your arms."

"Excuse me? This is ridiculous! I'm not -"

Teacher grabs sleeve, rolls it up, to reveal wounded arm.

I am silent.

Teacher is silent. Stares at arm.

"Can I go now?" I finally ask, pulling my sleeve down. Doing the whole I-can-cope-leave-me-alone routine.

Teacher doesn't know what to say. I am discussed in the staffroom. Everyone is distressed, preferably bringing up the fact that they don't understand how such a smart, mature girl could be doing this to herself. Add "pretty" to the list, even, if you want.

Of course, if that actually happened, they'd call in my parents. I assume. If they would even care that a student is engaging in self-destructive behaviours. And then they'd *know.*

And despite various brief fantasies in which I wave my cuts in front of their faces in a demand to be taken seriously, I don't want them to know.

They'd be disappointed in me, or disgusted with me, or something. They wouldn't understand me. And it's not like they understand me now, but they *think* they do. They think I'm a normal human being, someone they can connect with. Someone like *them*, someone who just gets on with life instead of whining about her feelings.

And if they knew the real me, they wouldn't love her.

Chapter Forty-Six

Wednesday evening and I'm hanging out at Sarah's house with her and Fiona. Why am I not at home being my usual introverted self, reading a book or organising my CDs into alphabetical order or fantasising about being on *Oprah* after I win a Pulitzer? Because Shane is coming over and she wants us there so that it's not too intimate and possibly embarrassing. I think it's ridiculous. She's been with him alone before, but I suppose now that she likes him and thinks he likes her, it's a little awkward.

I'm glad Fiona's here too, because at least then I'm not Third Wheel Girl.

And I'm really hoping that Sarah was being truthful when she said that they weren't going to talk shop, that they're just hanging out. Because if they start discussing the band, I'm leaving. Diving out the window, if I have to.

The Wonder Boy arrives. Says hi to us all. He still looks cute. If only I was pretty. If only I didn't have this overwhelming urge to lock myself away from the rest of the world to protect them from my hideousness.

We watch TV for a while, but once *The Simpsons* is over, there's nothing good on. I jokingly suggest that we play Scrabble. Shane says, "Actually - that might be fun."

I smile. "Are you serious?"

"Yeah. I love Scrabble."

I'm still not sure if he's just making fun of me or not, but we wind up getting it out and playing the game. Scrabble. These are my wild teenage years. And I am playing Scrabble.

I'm competitive at first and trying to impress Shane with my extensive vocabulary, and he's coming up with all these big long words that Sarah insists on checking in the dictionary to make sure they're real.

"And it's neck and neck between Abi and Shane as they battle for the title of Champion Scrabble Player!" Fiona says dramatically.

"Shane's going to win," Shane informs her.

"Shane's not going to win," I smile sweetly.

He narrows his eyes. "You think you can beat me."

"I'm going to try," I reply, equally solemnly.

He grins. (I swoon. Well, not quite, but I am gradually transformed from cynical dedicated Scrabble player to weak-at-the-knees infatuated groupie.)

Neither of us wins. Sarah and Fiona, who are

trailing behind, and who are fed up with the game at this stage, decide that cheating is the way to go.

"There you go!" Sarah says triumphantly after she's placed ten letters on the board.

Fiona is sorting through the rest of the letters, looking for an M.

"Here, have mine," Shane offers. And thus endeth the game as an actual game, if you follow me. Which is good because this way no one wins, and anyway I was in the lead before it started becoming a joke.

Not that it matters, of course.

Just to me.

And the best part of the whole night? Apart from feeling comfortable around Shane? And seeing him smile?

He didn't act *too* interested in Sarah. Maybe there's still hope . . .

Chapter Forty-Seven

I find myself listening to mushy love songs and/or stalker anthems. Bob Geldof's *Crazy*. The Police's *Every Breath You Take*. U2's *With or Without You*. The Goo Goo Dolls's *Iris*. Oasis's *Wonderwall*. Cyndi Lauper's *Time After Time*. Savage Garden's *Truly*

Madly Deeply. A whole collection of songs that remind me of love, that make me sigh happily.

Watch me be a ditzy teenage girl in love. Wait, not love. I'm not that deluded yet. It's just a crush. But crushes are fun. They're giddy and silly and melodramatic. You keep replaying moments in your mind. Like him smiling at me. There's this little spark of hope that he likes me, and it's enough to make me go around grinning like an idiot.

It's like someone's turned on the light and illuminated everyone's good points. Because on Thursday, my class don't bother me. At all. I've been too harsh. They're lovely, really.

Of course I know that my semi-ecstatic state has been brought about purely by Shane, and that everyone hasn't suddenly become much friendlier and interesting, but since I prefer being in a good mood, I'm not going to complain.

Shane Shane Shane!

Chapter Forty-Eight

For every action, there is an equal and opposite reaction.

For every day spent being deliriously happily because you think you have a chance with someone, there must be a day spent feeling far too hideous ever to be seen as attractive.

I feel ugly. More than that, though - I feel boring. Uninteresting.

I'm out of my league, a little girl pretending to be grown-up. Sarah fits in perfectly with Shane and his crowd. I don't. I'm *dull*. I spend too much time watching TV and reading and writing unreadable poetry. They're out living life, *doing* something, and I'm watching from the sidelines.

I don't even have an interesting past. No child-hood traumas lurking in my life, and it's not like I *want* to have them, but I feel less - valid for having a moderately happy upbringing. Like I'm a spoiled brat with no idea about pain or problems or anything that people in the "real" world have to face, like I've been sheltered and therefore have no right to feel anything, like I'm naïve and stupid and completely, utterly self-indulgent if I dare to feel depressed.

It's like you need proof, otherwise you're just being melodramatic. Of course, even when you get the proof, you still feel like you're an attention-seeker. Only, an attention-seeker who doesn't *get* any attention. An attention-seeker who's so reluc-tant to be seen as an attention-seeker than she does-n't seek it at all, but still wants it.

Everyone else with problems has *real* problems. Sarah's parents split up. Fiona took an overdose when she was thirteen. I want those problems. I want to have an eating disorder. I want to be diagnosed as having a chemical imbalance in my brain. I want to be told that I matter, that I'm not completely irrelevant.

I want Shane to cradle me in his arms and to be my protector and/or therapist. I want him to stroke my hair and I want him to dry away my tears.

You know that Sarah's the only one who's ever seen me cry? Not even my parents. I always hid from them when I was crying, racing up to my room before they could see tears fall. I couldn't let them see. It was too personal, too private.

Maybe it's the way our culture views crying as a sign of weakness. Maybe I'm nothing more than a product of media-and-family-imprinted messages. *Never cry keep it all bottled up don't bother anyone else with your problems because no one wants to hear it.*

Maybe it's just that I'm genetically doomed to be weird. I was born, and my parents knew I was different, but were in denial about it, because they were secretly hoping that it was just a horrible mistake and that I'd really turn out to be a normal, well-adjusted child. One who follows trends or one who plays sports. Not one who mopes about and spends far too much time dwelling on her life, which is a completely worthless endeavour, unless you're trying to depress yourself further, in which case it usually works.

Right. Quit moping. Think happy thoughts, like chocolate ice cream and the fact that *Frasier* is on tonight.

Chapter Forty-Nine

Saturday morning, I feel like shopping. My mom's going into town, so she agrees to give me a lift in.

I don't call Sarah or Fiona. I just want to go and buy books and CDs and then go home and enjoy them. Going into town with your friends means going for cups of coffee, chatting, hanging around. It's a day-long activity.

All I want to do is slink around the shops quietly and leave when I'm finished.

Of course, you know what they say about the best-laid plans of mice and men.

Actually, I *don't* know what they say. No one ever finishes off that quote. But I assume that it's something about the aforementioned plans being horribly derailed.

Anyway. Shane is in town. I see him in HMV just as I'm about to leave and he smiles at me. I go and say hi.

"What're you looking at?" I enquire, hoping it's not something too obscure.

He holds up Jeff Buckley's *Grace*.

"Buy it," I tell him.

He grins. "Is that an order?"

"Yes," I smile. "No CD collection is complete without it."

"That's what everyone seems to be telling me," he says.

"You should listen to them. Forget about individuality. Be a sheep! Buy it!"

He laughs. "OK, I'll follow the crowd. Just once." Pause. "Are you meeting up with someone now, or do you want to go get coffee or something?"

"Coffee sounds good," I smile.

(Yeah, you bet it does.)

So much for me being anti-social. I silence the part of me that still wants to go home and curl up with a book, and listen to the part that's telling me that this is my chance with Shane.

If he's even worth the effort. If any of this is worth the effort. If it isn't just easier to hide.

We go to one of those places with about a hundred different types of coffee on the menu, so many that it makes you dizzy just thinking about it. In the end I order tea, and he gets coffee. Plain, black coffee. It seems to confuse the waitress.

"So," he says, patting his HMV bag, "this is good, yeah?"

I nod. "Yep. Brilliant. He's got an incredible voice. Well, had."

"Such a tragedy he died so young," he intones solemnly. "Although I'm sure it did wonders for the record sales."

I grin. "Probably, yeah. The tragic-hero thing always goes down well. But it is actually good music."

"What did you buy?" he asks.

I hold up the CDs. *Boys For Pele* by Tori Amos, *Disintegration* by the Cure, *Boy* by U2.

"I approve," he smiles. "Especially the U2 one."

"Surprise, surprise."

Our tea and coffee are brought over. Shane watches, fascinated, as I pour the whole jug of milk into my cup.

"Have you ever thought about just getting milk?" he asks innocently.

"Oh, shut up."

"Aren't we very defensive about our tea-drinking habits?" he teases.

"Yes. I take my tea very seriously," I inform him.

"I can see that."

Pause.

Ask him does he like Sarah. Go on. You know you want to. Or tell him that you heard he likes someone in your school. Or get onto the subject of who he's interested in somehow. Without it looking incredibly obvious.

Why can't I just do this? Why can't I just ask him,

and find out, without making a big deal of it? Why do I feel so completely irrelevant around him? Maybe not even irrelevant, but just -

Not cool enough. That's it. So much for all my be-yourself-and-forget-about-what-anyone-else-thinks philosophy. When it comes down to it, I still think everyone else is superior to me and that I'm never going to be good enough.

This realisation annoys me. A lot.

"Do you like Sarah?" I ask him, my frustration at my own inferiority complex fuelling me.

He looks surprised. "Why do you ask?"

I shrug. "Just wondering. You seem to."

"She's great," he says. "She's fantastic, she's a really good friend and all, but . . . I don't know. I never really thought about her in that way."

"Fair enough," I nod.

Stay calm, stay calm, try not to give into the urge to leap out of your chair and scream 'I still have a chance!'

Chapter Fifty

We go our separate ways, Shane to see his friends, me to my bus stop. He asked me if I wanted to hang around with them, but I said that I didn't want to intrude. Which was true, and which means that I now get to go home and be reclusive.

And think about him. Should I have stayed in

town with him? He did invite me to, but then again, maybe he was just being polite. He was really in there to see his friends, after all. But what if he thinks that I said no because I don't like being around him? What if he thinks I hate him, and starts to feel resentful towards me because of it?

I muse about these things on the way home, coming down from the high of spending time with him and ending up feeling - well, extremely depressed. I write Shane's initials in the condensation on the window, then rub them off angrily.

Is that Graham getting on? Oh, fantastic. Just what I need. Hopefully he'll stay downstairs. No, of course he won't, he'll come up here.

Told you.

"Hey," he says. "Can I sit?"

I shrug. "Sure." It being a public bus and all.

"Are you OK?" he asks.

And oh God, it's stupid, but the way he asks, with this gentleness in his voice, makes me want to cry.

"Yeah," I say.

"Are you sure?"

I nod. "Positive."

"Look, if you ever need to talk . . ." He sighs. "OK, I know we're not on the best of terms at the moment, but I still want to stay friends with you."

"OK, whatever," I say quietly. I can't do this now, Graham, I can't argue with you. I'm just going to quietly agree with you and hope that you don't press the issue, because I can't handle it. I'm drained.

"Whatever?" he echoes.

"I'm agreeing with you, Graham. It's a good thing," I tell him.

We sit in silence for the rest of the bus journey, exchange "see ya"s, and then return to our lives.

I think about him asking me if I was OK, and how grateful I am to have someone caring about me.

Even if it is someone so incredibly evil. I shouldn't forget that. I really shouldn't.

Chapter Fifty-One

Help me.

I find myself reading over my old journals, the diaries I kept when I was in Second and Third Year, before I became too lazy and unmotivated to continue. I read the one from when I first met Graham. The "wow" feeling of having such a great friend who you feel that you can trust completely.

And we were good friends, you know? He always cared. That's the thing about him. He cares. He really -

What am I *saying*? This is Graham, the guy I've devoted so much time to hating.

Could I have been wrong? Maybe I'm too cynical. Just because I'm selfish and self-absorbed and horrible doesn't mean that the rest of the world is.

People make mistakes. It doesn't make them bad people.

I turn the page.

The sun started hiding behind the clouds, and I was getting cold, so he made me put on his jacket. I mean, he insisted. It was warm and soft and soothing, like being wrapped in a blanket. It made me feel safe and loved. He'd **given** *me this feeling. It's stupid, but I loved him so much at that moment. Not in a romantic way, because it's* **Graham**, *you know, but in a friendly way, in the sort of way that tells me that I'm never going to let him out of my life, that we're going to stay close throughout school and college and marriage and children and all that crap. There are so few people I feel that way about, and it's just amazing to have one more in my life, you know?*

Chapter Fifty-Two

There are too many Mondays. And I think that if a scientific study was ever done, they would find that Mondays take far longer to get through than any other day of the week, thus explaining the way that by Monday evening it feels like several more days should have elapsed.

On Monday afternoon I am doing something

which I can't believe I'm doing, yet seems to make sense.

I'm going over to Graham's house after school.

I'm crazy.

There must be a part of me that knows what I'm doing is completely stupid, because I don't tell Sarah about it.

Of course, it's not like it's a big deal, so why bore her with the details? Besides, it's not like I have time to mention it at lunch or anything. Sarah and I sit outside with a big group, including Fiona, Caroline and a couple of the people who were at the party and who know the guys in the band. It's fun. Emily, Hugh's girlfriend, is one of those people who always have something intelligent to say but never make you feel inferior while doing so, and we talk about the human need to label people. She's cool in that offbeat way that I long to emulate, and I get a kick out of the fact that we click right away. I start to feel like an interesting, worthwhile human being.

Can this really be happening? Am I actually feeling something akin to happiness and contentment while in school?

So between this and the thoughts of seeing Graham later, it's a rather bizarre day.

We agreed on half four. I'm five minutes late, deliberately. Because, with the crazy attitude there is in this country about time, being on time would

be considered being early. In fact, being five minutes late is considered being early. But far more
acceptable than actually being on time, if you follow me. I don't want him thinking that I was des-
perate to see him. Casual is the keyword here.

And what am I doing? I'm not trying to impress
him. I hate people who change themselves in order
to impress people, and here I am doing exactly the
same thing. I'm such a hypocrite.

And I'm obsessing over five minutes.

He answers the door.

"Hey, come on in."

Chapter Fifty-Three

When we are being civil to each other, it is so
strangely like old times that it feels like we never
fought. Being friendly, talking about our day, talking about mutual friends and acquaintances and
enemies . . . it feels so weirdly *right*.

When he hugs me, I don't want to let go.

When I "accidentally" push up my sleeves in a
casual gesture and he asks about the marks on my
arm even though it hits him instantly what they
are, I love the concerned look on his face, I love that
someone gives a damn, I love that he makes me feel
special and worthy of attention.

And that's why that, when he leans in to kiss me, I don't turn away.

Chapter Fifty-Four

On a scale of one to ten, with one being completely sensible-decisions sane, ten being completely are-you-out-of-your-mind insane, how would you rank what you did today, Abi?

A part of me says that it's somewhere around a fifteen.

Another part of me says "Hmm. Two?"

Chapter Fifty-Five

Monday night is when I lie awake contemplating the events of the day. Tuesday morning is pretty much the same, only sitting in an uncomfortable plastic chair instead of lying in bed.

Am I just doing this because Graham stepped into my life just when I was moping about the Shane situation and I feel like he's my rescuer? Or does this actually make sense? Do I actually like Graham?

Kissing him wasn't unbearable, which is a point in his favour. I don't particularly like kissing anyway. I mean, it's pointless, it really is. There is so much more intimacy in little gestures, the fingertips running along your arm, the teeth nibbling on your neck. Kissing is just . . . well, not bad, but not brilliant, let's put it that way.

But if I really hated him, then I wouldn't have been able to go near him. Unless of course it's just that I've been so love-deprived for so long that I don't care who it is who's kissing me.

I'm not that sort of person, am I? Physical contact should not be *that* important to me. Only somehow whenever it happens, it becomes important.

We're really nothing but animals, when it comes down to it.

I wonder what would have happened if Anna hadn't arrived home and we decided to go out for a walk. (Holding hands.) How far it would have gone.

And what am I doing? There's one part of me that shudders at the memory of the two of us sprawled out on his couch making out, and another that loves it. It's Graham. And then it's *Graham*.

He *cares*. And that makes me feel worthwhile, relevant, fabulous.

Chapter Fifty-Six

"I can't believe it's only Tuesday. How the *hell* is it only Tuesday? Are they playing some horribly cruel joke on us or something?"

Fiona is spending her lunch-time ranting about the injustice of the working week. Sarah and I nod in sympathy.

"Come on, at least we're off on Friday," Sarah reminds her.

Easter holidays. Ah. Bliss.

"Speaking of which, we really should do something this weekend," Fiona says.

"Girly sleepover fun?" Sarah grins. "Awful cheesy teen movies and an unhealthy amount of chocolate . . ."

"Mmm," she says. "*Or* . . . we could go out."

"Go out? *Out*? Into the real world? Are you serious?" Sarah kids.

Fiona smiles. "I know, it's all terribly exciting and daring. But seriously, Saturday night, what d'you think?"

"Sure," I shrug. I suppose it won't be *that* bad . . . will it? And it's good to try new things, right? Try to experience as much as you can when you're young? I haven't gone out to a club in nearly a year, since last summer.

"Sarah?"

"Sure, where? Bearing in mind that you're the only one of us with an ID, by the way."

"Well, if we bring Hugh along, we can go into town - he knows one of the bouncers at some club. Plus he's kind of cute."

Sarah and I stare at her.

She giggles. "Oh, come on, he is."

"Yeah, he is, but he's with Emily," Sarah reminds her.

"I know, I know," she sighs. "He's still fun to look at, though."

I grin. "So we're dragging him along, yeah?"

"Yes, we're going to shamelessly use him," Fiona says. "Some of us more than others."

"Well, if he's coming, then Emily's coming," Sarah muses. "Shane might want to come along, too . . ."

The mention of his name makes me feel strange. Very strange. I'm not sure why. It's not jealousy, is it? No, it can't be. I'm over him. I must be. Graham. Think of Graham. I like him. He's soft and safe and soothing and comforting. Shane is unfamiliar territory. Shane has too much power over me. Shane makes me insecure and anxious and I worry about every little thing I do when I'm around him.

"Can I ask Graham?" I ask.

"Sure," Sarah says automatically, and then both she and Fiona stare at me. "Wait. *What*?"

"He might like to come," I say.

"Since when are you two even *speaking* to each other?" Sarah enquires. "I thought you hated him with a passion."

I shrug. "We were hanging out yesterday, and it was . . . just like old times." If the 'old times' had involved tonsil tennis, that is.

"So you're friends with him again?" Fiona says, looking bewildered.

"Yeah, pretty much." I shouldn't have mentioned him. They both think I'm out of mind. I probably am.

"That's great," Sarah smiles. "Ask him about Saturday, anyway. It'll be more fun if there's a big group of us going."

Even though she's smiling, I know she's wondering what's going on, why I'm suddenly friends with someone who I've professed my undying hatred for many times. It doesn't make sense. I *know* it doesn't make sense. Chalk it up to living in a crazy mixed-up world, I guess.

Chapter Fifty-Seven

I see him on Tuesday evening. Wednesday evening. Thursday evening. It always begins with a hug. Then we talk. Hug. Curl up together and kiss.

It's safe. I have his arms around me and I'm leaning against him and I can feel the warmth of his body and I know he likes me and wants me . . . and it's fantastic.

And I don't tell Sarah, or Fiona. I don't tell Jess, not that she'd care. I don't tell Sharon when I email her. I don't feel like talking about it.

I don't know why. Is it because I'm scared of what they'll think? That they'll judge me?

Why would they judge me? Am I doing something wrong?

I really don't want to think about it, any of it.

Chapter Fifty-Eight

Friday morning. Last day of school before the Easter holidays. I think about Graham. And Shane.

In my mind, Graham and I are dancing, really close, and I can see Shane looking hurt. Jealous. And I like it.

This is why I'm a horrible person. I want to make Shane jealous. But I do like Graham. I really do. I like being around him.

Oh, this is just a big mess. One colossal mess. I want to turn back time. I want to snap my fingers and zap both of them out of my life completely. I want to go home and sleep for the next two weeks or so.

I concentrate on other things. Like what I'm going to wear tomorrow. I am Typical Teenage Girl, wondering what to wear to impress her -

Not boyfriend. Almost-boyfriend.

Do I want him to be my boyfriend?

I hate being indecisive. I want to slap myself. I would, if I wasn't sitting in class right now. I'd probably get strange looks. Wait, don't I get those already? Stranger looks, then.

I stare at my watch, counting down the minutes to home time, when I can escape from school, if not my thoughts.

Chapter Fifty-Nine

I can't believe they gave us homework. Homework. In Fourth Year. Over the Easter holidays. This is truly evil.

I am bored on Friday night. I cut. Not badly. Just scraping the skin. It won't even leave scars. Why am I still doing this? I don't know.

I sit cross-legged on my bed. Nothing to do. I don't feel like doing the homework. I don't want to write. I glance at the Sylvia Plath journals and am too intimidated by the size to even attempt to read.

I daydream about Shane.

Yes, I am a horrible person. Yes, I am just using Graham. *Yes*, I deserve to feel guilty.

And I don't. I don't feel guilty. I don't feel anything at all in the way of remorse. It bothers me. I should feel guilty, right?

Why can't I feel guilty? Why can't my mind let me accept the fact that I have done something wrong and immoral and blatantly *stupid* and feel bad about it? Why do I just keep thinking about Shane?

Shane who is not interested in me. Because he could never be interested in me. Because I'm boring, and ugly, and self-indulgent (come on, you know you were thinking it), and stupid. And I wallow in self-pity. Look at me, wallowing!

He *could* like me. He *might*. And it's that little spark of hope that keeps me going, keeps me daydreaming and sighing happily and feeling giddy at the thought of him. I'm crazy about him. I really am.

Chapter Sixty

"Last night . . . really didn't go as planned," I tell Emily on Sunday morning.

She nods. "Yeah. I know how you feel." Gulps down aspirin. "I'm never drinking again."

"Really?"

"No," she laughs.

I grin.

"Abi?"

"Yeah?"

"I'm sorry about . . . last night."

I shrug. "It's no big deal."

"No, seriously. I know I kinda freaked you out, and I'm sorry for the awkwardness and everything."

"It's fine. Seriously."

"Please keep in mind that I was very, very drunk and promise to never kiss you ever again."

I smile. "That's very considerate, thank you."

She smiles. "That's me."

As you may have guessed, Saturday night was . . . somewhat eventful.

The drama began before we even left. We were all meeting up before going into town. Shane and Hugh had already been drinking. Graham looked disapproving and kept muttering things to me about them. How pathetic it was that they needed to drink before even going out. This was complete hypocrisy on Graham's part, by the way. He's done it himself many times. I think he was just feeling insecure. Compared to the other guys he seemed immature, a sulky brat. He even looked younger. I mean, there's only a year's difference between their ages, but they seemed almost grown-up, and he seemed still very much a child.

Of course I was trying not to think about this, because Graham had his arm around me and we were acting like a couple (which we were, I suppose, in a way) and it wouldn't have been the best time to mention that I was sort of madly in love with Shane. Besides, he'd asked me, the moment he saw me, how I was, how I felt, whether I was OK.

And yes, I'm a sucker for concern, OK?

We got into the club no problem. I couldn't help but smirk a little when I saw Leanne, Hannah and a couple of others being turned away while we got in.

Alcohol was ordered by all. I didn't intend drinking, but when Graham handed me a drink I decided just to go along with it. It wasn't peer pressure. Really. (Sure, Abi, keep telling yourself that . . .)

We danced. I object to dancing. I'm terrible at it. However, after a few drinks, I was wonderful. At least, I thought I was. And that's the important thing, right?

Graham clung to me like a leech. Oh, that sounds too harsh. Wait, no, it isn't, as you will soon learn. He wrapped his arms around me, pressed himself against me.

The others were still dancing in a group at this stage, along with a couple of other friends from

school. I noticed that Hugh and Emily weren't acting terribly couple-ish, not that I'd ever really seen
them act that way before, but it surprised me that
they barely seemed to even look at one another. I
mean, at Sarah's party they hadn't been one of
those sickeningly-cute permanently-glued-to-one-
another couples, but they hadn't avoided each
other, either.

Slow songs. Ah, what clears a dance floor faster
than a slow song? I was permanently attached to
Graham, of course, so there was no question of me
going to join the others and commiserate about our
terrible love lives and the depressing nature of slow
songs.

Now that I think about it, most of the others
wouldn't have been commiserating. I was swaying
slightly with Graham as I watched Hugh pull Fiona
over to dance. The strangeness of it jolted me. I
looked away -

- and found myself staring at Shane with some
girl. He had his hands cupping her face. I couldn't
see her properly. But I knew who it was. Of course
I knew who it was.

Don't stare, Abi, they might notice, I told myself.
So instead I just buried my face in Graham's
shoulder and tried not to cry. Gulp, gulp. Hold
back the tears. Don't let yourself cry. Not now. You
can't hurt Graham by crying on his shoulder over

another guy.

The song didn't help. It was - oh, I remember now. It was 'Iris'. And it hurt.

Chapter Sixty-One

I don't think I've ever been so relieved to hear a song end. After that, I just threw myself into the music, dancing away frantically.

Look at me now, Shane. Look at me enjoying myself. Watch me move to the music. Wish you could have me? Jealous of Graham? I don't need you. I can have fun without you.

Of course, if he'd come over to me at that moment and declared his undying love for me, I would have fallen at his feet. But he didn't. So I kept dancing.

With Graham.

I'd glance over at Shane and then look away in case he saw me looking. But I always knew where he was. By that stage our group had broken apart into fragments, individuals and couples floating around, and I'd lost track of everyone else. Except him.

And, because she was with him, Sarah. Naturally.

Sarah who's so pretty and kind and wonderful

and talented and of *course* he likes her. Who wouldn't?

We were supposed to be leaving at two. I came up with many innovative ways to look at my watch without it seeming like I was actually looking at my watch. Finally I told Graham that I needed fresh (fresh? In Dublin?) air, and that since it was half-one, I probably wouldn't bother coming back in.

He offered to come with me. Of course he did. That's what a good boyfriend-type-figure does.

I accepted, because I doubted that anything short of a severe blow to the head would prevent him from following me.

We left, me breathing in the gloriously polluted air, him stroking my back.

It was at that point that he started whining. Why couldn't I just have stayed inside for another while? We'd been having a great time dancing. Why had I bothered inviting him if I wasn't going to enjoy myself?

I stared at him, and I had an epiphany. I saw him, really saw him, for the first time since I'd seen him on the bus that day. I saw the whiny self-righteous brat, the manipulative asshole, the boy that had hurt me and was now doing it again, by making me feel horribly bad over something as silly as leaving a club early.

I had been using him. And he'd been using me. We both wanted someone to listen to us, to make us feel special. He didn't really care about me, which suited me just fine because I didn't really care about him.

"Graham," I said hesitantly, "I think we need to talk."

Chapter Sixty-Two

He didn't take it well.

Well, of course he didn't take it well. We are talking about *Graham*, after all. And in typical Graham-like fashion, he got angry at me.

He accused me of being incredibly screwed up and of using him. He said I'd taken advantage of his feelings for me. He told me I'd led him on.

And I said nothing. Only it wasn't because I couldn't think of anything to say. It was because he was completely and utterly right.

He stormed off, and I was left in tears on the street alone. Well, not alone as such. There were several drunken people there as well. I choose not to count them because I didn't know them and because most of them were barely conscious.

I took out my phone to call Sarah, only I realised I really didn't want to speak to her at the moment.

I called Fiona, but she didn't answer. Shockingly enough, it can be quite difficult to hear a mobile phone ring when music is blaring out of giant speakers.

I was drying my eyes when Emily walked out. "Abi! What happened?"

I sniffed. "Graham and I broke up."

"Oh, honey," she said sympathetically, hugging me. I almost didn't want to let go. It felt like she was the only person who cared about me at that moment, the only person in the entire world that thought that I mattered.

"It's OK," I told her. "I mean, I wasn't interested in him at all - I hate him, in fact - it's just that he has a tendency to yell at people when he's angry. It's not exactly fun."

"I bet. I hate people like that."

"You going back inside?" I asked.

She looked at her watch. "Nah, not going to bother. You want to go get a taxi home?"

In the taxi, I took out my phone to text Sarah.

"Who're you texting?" Emily asked.

"Sarah. I'm supposed to be sleeping over at her house tonight . . . but I don't think that's going to happen." I sounded just a *tad* bitter when I said that, I guess.

"You like Shane, huh?"

I nodded. "Yep."

"If it makes a difference . . . it seemed to me like he was only with Sarah tonight because he wanted to make you jealous. Which I suppose makes him an asshole for using Sarah like that . . . but I don't think he would have gone near her if you hadn't been with Graham tonight."

I sighed. "And I didn't even want to be with Graham tonight. This is messy. Very, very messy."

"So I see."

"What about you and Hugh? What happened there?"

She shrugged. "I have absolutely no idea. Well, I do, in a way. We all started dancing and I could tell he liked Fiona. He kept looking over at her, and she was in that little low-cut top and looked absolutely wonderful and all that, and I just got fed up with it and told him that if he wanted her, he should just go for it."

"Seriously?"

"What else could I say? I didn't want him to be with me because he felt he *had* to be. If he likes her, good for her. I hope they're very happy together."

"No, you don't."

"No, I don't," she agreed. "I hope they're absolutely miserable together, but that's beside the point."

"It could be just a one-night thing, though. I mean, people do crazy things when they're drunk."

"They weren't that drunk, though."

"I know. I was trying to make you feel better," I smiled.

She laughed. "I appreciate the effort."

Chapter Sixty-Three

"If you want to stay over at my house, you can," she said.

"You sure?"

"Yeah, sure. I'll find you a T-shirt or something to sleep in. We can paint each other's nails."

I laughed. "OK."

Well, it was either that or go home. And I was sobering up and feeling wide awake, and the thought of going home didn't really appeal to me. Besides, I could tell she was upset over Hugh, and I didn't want to leave her alone.

The sobriety became a moot point when we got back to Emily's and decided to finish off a bottle of wine that had been left in the fridge. And by finish off, I mean - well, start. And then move onto another bottle.

So there we were, in her bedroom, sitting on the floor, bitching about the general evilness of guys, and why they're so cruel and manipulative and completely not worth it, when she giggled and said, "See, what I *need* is a girlfriend."

"Ahhh," I said.

"I'm serious! I'm fed up with guys. They just screw you around - I'm so sick of it. But with girls - they're more gentle. Softer. They're *pretty*."

I still wasn't quite sure what to say here. While I was feeling quite bitter towards mankind at that moment, part of the bitterness was due to the fact that I still liked Shane, despite it all.

She turned to me. "I mean, look at you."

(Oh, let's not look at me. We don't need to look at me at all. Really.)

She stared at me for a moment. "You're . . . just fabulous. You're so beautiful. I don't think you even realise how beautiful you are."

Her hands were in my hair and her mouth was on mine before I knew it. We stayed like that for a few moments before I pulled away.

Emily looked at me, and hid her face in her hands. "Oh, God. Tell me I didn't just do that."

"You didn't just do that," I obliged.

"Abi, I'm sorry . . . I didn't mean to. Can we just forget this ever happened, completely ignore the fact that I've just made a fool of myself?"

"It's forgotten," I reassured her, while my mind was still wondering, *What just happened*?

Well, I knew what had just happened. Emily had kissed me. Which, because it was Emily, was flattering in a way, but at the same time, a little weird.

Stereotype

It wasn't just because she was a girl. At least, I don't think it was. It was just unexpected. It's always strange to be kissed by someone you're not attracted to, even if they are as fabulously cool as Emily.

We fell asleep soon after that, and woke up in the morning with lovely hangovers. Oh, the joys of being a teenager.

Chapter Sixty-Four

"Did you have a good night out?" the parents ask. I don't know why they ask. They don't want details. They don't want to know what's happening in my life.

"Yeah, it was OK," I reply. The right answer, the one they want to hear.

"Did you get much sleep? You look tired."

"Yeah, I am. I think I'll go up to bed for a while."

I lie in bed and contemplate the events of Saturday night, and the more I think about it, the more it starts to remind me of an over-the-top teen drama series.

I think about Shane and Sarah and, because I'm in the mood for torturing myself, put on *Iris*. And then I replay it.

And again. And again. And again.

Abi, I tell myself, you are absolutely pathetic.

You got yourself into this mess. You put the idea of liking Sarah into Shane's head. You invited Graham along and danced with him. This situation is entirely your own fault.

Somehow it doesn't make me feel better . . .

Chapter Sixty-Five

On Monday the sun is shining. I wear long sleeves. Town isn't particularly crowded, but it's still busy. People rush off to work. Rush to the shop for a doughnut or a cup of coffee. Rush, rush, rush. It's calmer inside the shops. Sales assistants stack new books on shelves, rearrange CDs, brush specks of dust off clothes, chat.

They eye me suspiciously as I browse. Oh, give me a break! Do I look like I'm going to steal something? Why do you assume that just because I'm a teenager I'm up to no good?

Fine. You want to think the worst about me? Go ahead. Might as well give you some evidence to back up your assumptions. I'll just slip this book into my bag and see if you notice. See if I can get away with it. Walk out.

No alarm wailing, no one stopping me. So easy. Sure, it's wrong. Do I care? Not really.

Or maybe I do, and maybe that's why I'm doing

it. But I'm not in the mood for in-depth self-analysis. I have shops to visit.

CDs are impossible to take. There's no use trying to steal them. Books are easy. Cosmetics are easy. Clothes can be, depending on the shop. Check for security tags, check for observant shop assistants.

Look casual. Look normal. Browse first, then take, then walk slowly out of there.

I go home and read. Jess yells at me over something trivial. I go into the bathroom and take out a razor-blade. Automatic reaction. Don't think; just do. What a life.

Chapter Sixty-Six

Tuesday brings with it a hate-filled text message from Graham, which I delete, and then switch off my phone in disgust. I don't want to talk to anyone. I just want to be left alone.

I toy with the idea of thrusting my scarred arms in front of my parents' faces and saying "Look!" Keeping it a secret doesn't seem to matter any more. Who cares if they know?

And yet I know that I'm never going to tell them. There's a power in being secretive, a feeling of control over your life when you and only you know what's really going on.

And now I've added shoplifting to the list of Typical Teenage Things that I've done. I paint my nails in a shade of dark blue, courtesy of Boots and the distracted sales assistants.

I hate waiting for nail varnish to dry. It is the dullest of dull activities. You can't move. Because if you move, you'll smudge the nail varnish, undoing all the work that went into painting each nail carefully and perfectly. Forget about burning bras and not shaving your legs, the feminist movement needs to start thinking about the nail varnish conspiracy. What better way to keep women oppressed than by nail varnish? While waiting for it to dry, we're rendered immobile. It chips easily, so we're forced to reapply it at regular intervals, or else buy overcoats and undercoats and all that sort of thing, which diverts our funds away from important things, leaving us dependent on our boyfriends/partners/husbands, taking away our power so that we're at their mercy.

It's a valid theory. I'm not insane. Really.

Someone's at the door. I'm the only one at home, unfortunately, so I'll have to journey all the way downstairs to answer it instead of yelling at one of my siblings to answer it. It's probably one of their friends, anyway. One of Jess's friends, trying to look rebellious and cool in a Korn hoodie, hands shoved in the pockets of impossibly baggy trousers, or one of Greg's friends, with a football tucked under his arm.

I'm wrong. It's Sarah. "Heya. Can I come in?"

"Sure," I say. "What's up?" Because *something's* up if she's asking can she come in, without waiting for me to invite her, or even just walking in because she knows that she doesn't need an invitation.

"Are you OK with me and Shane?" She gets straight to the point.

"Yeah," I lie. It's what she wants to hear. She's not here to find out whether I'm actually OK with it or not. She's here to ask, to be told that everything's OK, so she can go on her merry way with a clear conscience.

"Seriously. Are you? I know you said you didn't like him, but I had a feeling you did. And then you invited Graham along and spent the night with him and I figured that you didn't like Shane after all, but now . . . I don't know. I wanted to make sure you're not upset about this."

"I'm fine with it, really. So what exactly is the story with you two? Are you going out with him?"

She grins. "Yeah."

I smile. She looks so happy.

"So, what about you and Graham, huh?" she enquires.

"Oh. Yeah," I say somewhat unenthusiastically.

"Well . . . is he your boyfriend now, or what? You

seemed pretty close on Saturday night."

"Yeah, but . . . then I came to my senses. He's an asshole. He hasn't changed."

She breathes a sigh of relief. "Oh, thank God. I was thinking you'd completely lost your mind there for a second, and I was going to have to pretend to like the guy for your sake."

"Nope. He's out of my life forever. Hopefully."

"Fabulous." She hugs me. "Well, listen, I'd better go - I'm supposed to be meeting Shane at three, so . . ."

"Have fun," I say.

She beams. "I'm sure I will."

Chapter Sixty-Seven

Jealousy. It feels like I spend most of my life being jealous. Of Sarah, who's so perfect, who's so wonderful, who everyone loves. Of the pretty girls. Of the smart girls. Of the talented girls.

Can't I just step out of my skin and be one of them? Can't I be special too?

Can't someone I like ever reciprocate the feeling? Unrequited love isn't fun. It's painful. It's depressing. Do people ever really find people to love who love them in return, or do they end up settling? Did my parents fall madly in love, or did they decide that it was better to be married than live alone?

I mope. I mope and I mope and I mope, and I'm so sick of it, so sick of myself, so sick of everything. I wish I could sleep but don't want to. I wish I could distract myself by watching TV, but it doesn't work. I wish I could write something, but I can't. My mind's blank. I'm frustrated. I'm bored.

Boredom. That's what it is, Abi. It's not depression or anything as interesting or valid as you'd like to believe. It's just you being fed up.

You're not special. There's nothing unique about you. You're just a silly little girl, a melodramatic teenager who wants so badly to believe that she's important that she has scars in an attempt to prove it. Grow up.

Chapter Sixty-Eight

I'm in town again on Wednesday. I wander aimlessly around, slipping into shops I've never visited before, seeing what I can get away with.

"Heya," a blue-haired girl says, stopping in front of me on Grafton Street. It takes me a moment to recognise her as Emily.

"Hey! Love the hair." It really does look fabulous, making her stand out from the crowd. I debate dying my own hair, then decide that it's unique enough already without adding dye. Maybe auburn isn't such a bad colour after all.

She grins. "Thanks. What're you doing in town?"

I shrug. "Shopping."

"Ah, right. Get anything nice?"

"Not really. Just looking around."

"Well, listen, there's a few of us over in Stephen's Green, if you feel like sitting down and listening to Hugh try to sing. He has a guitar - there's no stopping him!"

"Can he sing?"

"No," she laughs. "It's a nightmare. But we're having fun."

"Who else is there? Anyone I know?" I ask.

"Well, Fiona, but she's busy telling Hugh how wonderful he is." She rolls her eyes. "You know Barry? Roisín? Andrew?"

"Vaguely," I say. They were at Sarah's party, but I didn't really speak to any of them.

"Good enough," she grins.

"I think I'm going to go home, actually," I say, shying away from the possibility of actually interacting with other human beings. More to the point, human beings I barely know.

"Not in a social mood, huh?"

I nod. "Yeah."

Stereotype

"OK. Well, I'll see ya - sometime, I'm sure. Take care of yourself."

"You too."

I watch her walk away. I want her to come back. I thought she wanted to be friends, that she actually cared about me. *No, Abi, she doesn't really give a damn. She just fancied you. Get over it.*

And then I remind myself that she invited me to hang out with her friends, and that I refused. Because I'm not in the mood to be social. But I still feel left out.

I am the epitome of unreasonable and irrational. I know, I know.

To make my day even better, I pass by Shane and Sarah kissing. On the street. I hate people who can't keep their hands off each other in public. They're so wrapped up in each other that they don't notice me.

I would yell out 'Get a room!' but I'm too choked up to speak without bursting into tears.

I go home, slam the door behind me, storm up to my room, throw myself on the bed and cry. Every time I stop crying, I keep reminding myself of everything that's so awful in my life, and it starts all over again.

And then finally it stops, and I get up, dry my eyes.

I roll up my sleeves, stare at my arms. I empty out my bag, the bottles of nail varnish and lipsticks and earrings and key-rings falling onto the bed.

The cliché, the angry teenager who overreacts to everything and acts out to get attention, the thing I never wanted to become, is what's standing in my room right now. Where did I go?

I'm like the rest of them, thinking that I'm different, special, unique, when I'm not. We're synchronised swimmers, moving in perfect unison. We like to think we're doing something different, but it's just part of the routine. When we look around we realise everyone else is doing exactly the same thing.

I don't know how to be different. I can keep cutting, keep stealing, keep wallowing in my pathetic little teenage angst, and that won't make me special. I can be happy and well-adjusted, and that still won't make me special. I can work hard in school or I can fail, and it won't make any difference; it's all been done before.

Everything has been done before.

So what does that leave? I ask myself.

Chapter Sixty-Nine

I make a list. Reasons why I feel depressed.

I'm ugly and uninteresting.

Everyone else isn't.

I feel like no one cares about me.

I feel like no one takes me seriously.

I feel like a typical teenager, and that annoys me, because I want to be special.

I cut myself. But that isn't really a reason. More a consequence.

I don't have any valid reasons. That bothers me more than anything. I can't really put my finger on why I feel like this. It's too vague and non-specific.

Because there's a part of me that likes feeling down. I like being the victim in my own mind. It means I can wallow without actually doing anything about it.

My life feels pointless.

The words 'brat' and 'self-indulgent' come to mind. I crumple up the list. I throw things around my room. Shoes hit walls. CD cases crack. By the time I calm down, the room is a mess. Well, more of a mess.

I take out an old notebook and begin to write. Words spill out of me, angry, depressed, sad, bitter, lonely. I don't censor myself in an attempt to sound deep and meaningful. I don't toss in any symbolism to make it sound more poetic. I just write, because I need to, I need to get this out of me and isn't it better to get it out through writing than through blood?

I write about hating the people at school even though I used to want to be like them, about how

Sarah and Shane being together is painful and beautiful at the same time, about feeling empty and maybe now sickened over Graham.

How can you let your worst enemy touch you just because they pretend to care? How can you sink that low and not even realise it? How can you tolerate someone's company just so you can feel validated? I used him because he paid attention to me, and I ignored Sarah, who actually gives a damn, maybe because it's always easier to reveal your secrets to someone whose opinion doesn't matter . . .

My hand gets tired after a while. I turn on the radio instead. Poppy, happy music is playing. Total teenybopper stuff. I listen anyway. It's light, it's bubbly, it's fun.

I start cleaning up my room. It feels oddly calming, like I'm taking control. Which I guess I am. Yes, I decide. I am taking control. I'm going to stop moping. I know it can't possibly be that simple, but I have to try. I'm sick of living like this.

I text Sarah asking if she wants to sleep over tomorrow night. I doubt the parents will have any objections, and we haven't properly talked in a while.

I set my phone aside, expecting her to be too engrossed in Shane to reply, but a beep two minutes later proves me wrong.

Sure, would love to! What time will I come over?

Stereotype

Chapter Seventy

I'm still in that I-feel-powerful-and-I-can-take-control-of-my-life state of mind as I go to bed.

I dream about Shane. He arrives at my house and tells me that he's not with Sarah any more, that it was unfair to her when he's in love with me.

I am deliriously happy, walking on air, grinning idiotically. I can't believe this is happening to me, that my wildest dreams are coming true.

Then I wake up and realise that it really is just a dream. It hurts. I want to recapture it, slip back into the dreamland where everything is perfect.

I feel like stamping my foot down on the ground and demanding to know why? Why is it that I'm doomed to live a life without reciprocated love?

And why must I be so melodramatic about it?

I lie in bed thinking about him. We don't have much in common, really, I remind myself. He's idealistic and pretentious. (And gorgeous.) The only reason I want him is because I think it's never going to happen. I need someone to daydream about, and he'll do.

It's not working. I can't convince myself that I don't have feelings for him, because I do. And I don't know how to stop feeling like this. You can't control your emotions.

I think about cutting and then turn over in bed

angrily. No. I'm fed up with doing that, fed up with having to hide the scars, fed up with being such a cliché.

I read a little Sylvia Plath before realising that I'm trying *not* to be depressed, and go downstairs and watch cartoons instead. *As Told By Ginger* is on, keeping me entertained for half an hour. I keep reliving the Shane-dream during the ad breaks, filling up with a longing for the unattainable.

Chapter Seventy-One

She looks pretty. As always. Perfect and pretty and why can't I be like that?

She has that glow, that happy-in-love glow, about her. I'm jealous. I almost hate her for having Shane, for being so *happy*.

I'm trying to stay happy and positive and optimistic. But I don't get it. I don't understand how people survive in a world that's so unfair.

I make the mistake of asking how things are going with Shane. We're in my room, listening to the Foo Fighters, sitting on the bed, and she says, "He's kinda possessive."

"Really?" I say.

"Yeah, I don't like it. I mean, he's great and all, don't get me wrong, but I wish he'd loosen up."

"Well, if you don't like it, you can always break up with him," I say. It sounds more bitter than I meant it to be.

She looks at me strangely. "Abi, what's your problem?"

"Nothing! Just . . ."

"Just *what*?"

"Just that I can't believe you're complaining about him already! I mean, do you have any idea how lucky you are to be going out with him? And already you're moaning about how possessive he is."

"So much for you not liking him," she mutters.

"Oh, screw you, Sarah! If you knew me at all you'd have known I was still crazy about him."

"Maybe that's the problem! I *don't* know you. You never tell me anything! I don't know why you do the things you do. I mean, you and Graham. What the hell was with that?"

"At least he actually *gives* a damn about me, unlike some people."

"Oh, grow up! The only reason he's nice to you is because he wants to sleep with you."

"Get out. Get out of here right now."

"Gladly," she says coldly, grabbing her bag and storming out of the room. She closes the front door firmly, not quite loud enough to be a slam, but close enough.

I want to cry. I want to throw things. I want to slice at my arms until the blood turns into a river. I want to turn the world inside out, smash windows, start fires, kill people.

I cry first. Floods of tears. I can't picture them ever stopping. I've never felt so alone, never been so alone. Unloved, unwanted, uninteresting. The rest of my life will be spent alone, living like a hermit, living like a crazy poet, and now that there's an excellent chance of that dream becoming reality, it scares me. I don't want that. I don't want to be cut off from the world. I need my friends, I need to feel needed and valued.

Instead I'm just a petty self-indulgent whiny child, and everyone knows it, everyone has seen the real me, and they hate her. I don't blame them. I'd hate me too. I do hate me. I hate who I am. I don't know how I can change, if it's even possible. I want to sleep and forget it all, but I don't think I can.

I need a fairy godmother to tell me what to do. I need Sarah to come back and tell me that she's sorry and that she still wants to be friends with me. I need Shane to confess his undying love for me. I need my parents to tell me that they think I need counselling. I need a hug.

And then the phone rings.

Chapter Seventy-Two

The music is pounding out of the speakers. It feels like it's pounding in time with my heart. I dance. I dance crazily and wildly, possibly because I'm a little drunk. Emily's friend Barry and a couple of other guys are dancing with me. One of them spins me around. I almost fall and he catches me. I giggle. He grins.

I catch Sarah looking over and glare defiantly at her. It's like the night she and Shane got together. Let them do whatever they want. I can still have a good time. And I am. I feel pretty. Desirable.

Emily comes over and joins us. "Hey, everything OK?" she asks me.

"Yeah," I reply.

"Have you been talking to Sarah yet?"

"No, she's too busy with her darling Shane."

Emily makes a face. "Don't let it bother you. Just have fun."

"I'm trying," I grin.

She laughs, and takes my hands. We twirl around, *Titanic*-style. The guys watch in appreciation. I get dizzy and slip. We both fall to the ground, giggling hysterically.

"OK, how much have you had to drink?" Barry asks, playing the part of the concerned older brother figure.

"Just a little," I giggle.

"Yeah, right," Emily says.

"Look who's talking," I say, sticking my tongue out at her.

"Don't stick that tongue out at me unless you intend to use it," she laughs.

I raise my eyebrows.

As do the guys. "Can we watch?" one of them asks.

Emily gives him the finger.

I try to get up, but fail miserably, falling back down on the ground beside Emily. She looks at me and suddenly I'm thinking *Oh what the hell* and I'm kissing her and even though my eyes are closed I know the guys are watching.

She pulls away. I open my eyes. Talk about making a scene. It feels like the whole room's staring at us. Sarah, Shane, Hugh, Fiona, Caroline, surprised and shocked in a terribly politically incorrect way. Barry and the other guys, looking as if they'd like us to continue, preferably with clothes removed. Emily's friend Roisín, smiling.

She gets up off the ground and helps me up. Ignoring the stares, she dances. I follow her cue. I feel like she's waiting to tell me something. A few minutes later she slips outside, indicating for me to follow.

"I'm not your toy, Abi," she tells me.

Stereotype

"Excuse me?" I'm confused. Nothing to do with the alcohol or anything, oh no.

"Nice little show you put on there for everyone," she says. "But for God's sake, Abi, if you're looking for a co-star, find someone else to use. Don't mess around with me, OK?"

"I wasn't -" I protest feebly.

She shoots me a I-know-you're-lying-so-cut-the-crap look.

"OK," I say softly. "Are you mad at me?" *Please don't be mad . . .*

She relents and smiles. "Nah. You're too damn cute."

"Aw, thanks," I laugh.

"Come on, let's go back inside," she says, then pauses. "You know, they're probably all in there thinking we're out here screwing . . ."

Chapter Seventy-Three

Vodka shots. Ah, sure, why not?

"Abi, you sure that's a good idea?" Emily says.

"Yes, I think it's a great idea," I reply. *Since when are you my mother? I don't need to be looked after.*

She shrugs. "OK . . ."

I'm annoyed. Just to spite her, I pour out another one and gulp it down. The taste isn't so bad after a

157

while. But it's still pretty disgusting. I go into the kitchen to find something to get rid of the taste still lingering in my mouth.

One of the guys I was dancing with earlier - is it Declan? - is in there, opening up a can of beer. "Heya," he says.

"Hey," I respond, opening the fridge. Orange juice. That'll do.

"Aren't we very healthy?" he observes as I pour myself a glass.

"Need to get the taste of vodka out of my mouth," I explain.

He grins.

"OK, so I'm not exactly a hardened drinker," I admit.

"So why don't you stick to alcopops?" he asks.

I shrug. "They don't work fast enough."

He's amused. "You're a bit of an alcoholic, aren't you?" he smiles.

"Oh yeah. After this I've got my AA meeting," I laugh. I try to casually sit up on the table, and slip off. Way to go, Abi.

"You're a little drunk," he notes.

"I am not," I reply indignantly.

He looks at me sceptically.

"Maybe just a little," I relent.

"So . . . what's the deal with you and Emily?" he asks.

"Deal?"

"Well . . . you were meeting her earlier. Are you with her or what?"

"We're friends," I say.

He raises his eyebrows. "Yeah, I always act that way with my friends."

"We're friends who seem to end up kissing whenever we're drunk. That's about it."

"I *see*."

"I don't know why I did it. I guess because I know she likes me, and I like that, you know? I mean, we all like to feel desirable, right? I think she's cool, yeah, but I'm not interested in her. I'm straight. I just . . . I don't know." I sit down at a chair and put my head on the table. "I don't know! Aaaagh! I don't know why I do these things! I do such stupid things, you know?"

He nods, taking a seat beside me. I notice he's got a burn-mark on his hand. "How'd you get that?" I ask, touching it gently.

He shrugs. "Cigarette-burn."

"You smoke?"

"Yeah. I know, I know, it's bad for my health and all that crap."

I shrug. "We all have our self-destructive habits."

He nods like I've said something incredibly wise. "So what's yours?"

"Apart from being an alcoholic?" I laugh.

"Yeah, apart from that."

I shrug. "Sharp things."

He gets it. Of course he gets it. I'm willing to bet he burned himself on purpose, that he's got more marks hidden.

"Let's see," he says.

I push up my sleeve and I can tell he's impressed and disgusted at the same time. There are fresh cuts, still crimson and raw and swollen, and then there are scabs, broken dark red lines, and scars, dark pink, fading but not quite gone, definitely making their presence known.

I'm right about him. Because then he shows me his cigarette-burns going all the way up his arm.

"Not as bad as yours, though," he says.

The tone of his voice gets to me, for some reason. "It's not a competition," I say, but I don't think he believes me. Suddenly I don't want him looking at me, if he's just trying to see who's worse off. It feels too twisted, even for me.

I pull my sleeve down. Safe again. He follows suit.

"Why'd you do it?" I ask him.

He shrugs. "I don't know. Sometimes you just need to hurt yourself to make yourself feel something. And sometimes you feel too much."

"And sometimes you're just looking for attention, right, Declan?" Emily says, pushing the door open.

"Emily!" I can't believe she's just said that. I didn't realise she was such a heartless bitch.

"It's not like that," Declan protests.

She looks at him tiredly. "No, of *course* it isn't," she snaps.

I'm starting to feel sick. I stand up, and it makes me feel worse. Head-rush combined with an onslaught of nausea.

"Abi?" Emily sounds concerned.

"I'm going to go . . ." I indicate the door.

"Are you OK?"

I nod. "Yeah, I'm . . . no."

"Do you feel sick?"

"Kinda." The nausea hits me even worse. I move towards the door. I don't seem to be that good at moving.

"Here, come on," Emily says, propelling me out the door and in the direction of the bathroom. I kneel down in front of the toilet and throw up. It feels almost religious. The kneeling, I mean. Like confession, or doing your penance afterwards. *Forgive me, Father, for all my sins . . .*

She's holding my hair back from my face and rubbing my back and I'm thinking, *What the hell have I done to deserve a friend who'll watch me throw up after I've messed with her head.* Then I think about what she said to Declan, and it hurts. Is that what she thinks it's all about? Getting attention?

Isn't it?

Chapter Seventy-Four

"I'm never drinking again," I vow.

"Don't make promises you can't keep," Emily warns.

It is the morning after. Emily, me, and assorted other people, excluding Declan, are having breakfast, sprawled across the floor of the sitting-room and the kitchen. Or trying to have breakfast, anyway. I can't eat much. This would be what they refer to as a bad hangover. Actually, this is what they refer to as a *monster* hangover, the kind that feels like it's going to cling to you forever, like the nausea's never going to leave and you're never going to be able to eat ever again, or think clearly, for that matter, because you've got people with sledgehammers bashing away from inside your skull, and it really, *really*, really hurts.

It kills me to admit it, but I find myself thinking that my parents have the right idea. Damn. I was trying to rebel.

Emily goes to make us tea, good hostess that she

is. Roisín sits down beside me and asks me if I'm OK.

"Yeah, I think so," I reply. "I will be, anyway."

She smiles. "I know how you feel." She pauses. "Mind if I ask you something personal?"

"Go ahead," I say, although I'm nervous. I'm not good with discussing anything personal. And I don't know her that well. But she's friendly, and maybe I've got to stop thinking that I need to have people's life histories before opening up to them.

"What's the deal with you and Emily?"

I feel like I've been down this road before. Oh, wait, I was, last night. I'm not sure what to say this time. I get the feeling whatever I say will be repeated to Emily later.

"We're friends," I say.

"Friends who kiss."

"Once."

"Twice." She smiles. "Yeah, she told me. Look, Abi, she likes you. I don't know if it's a rebound thing or what, but she *does* like you. And you shouldn't take advantage of that."

"I know," I say softly. "I feel really crappy about it." I think I'm about to cry. And I think she knows, because she looks at me sympathetically.

"Don't beat yourself up over it too much. We all have drunken moments that we regret."

"Have you got any?" I ask.

Claire Hennessy

She muses. "Well, I got into a fight with Fiona last night and called her a fat slut, but apart from that . . ."

I laugh. "No way!"

"I know! It's awful!" She hides her face in her hands. "I can't believe I just told you that. She's one of your best friends, isn't she?"

"Yeah, she is. But I haven't really spoken to her since she got together with Hugh."

"You're avoiding her?"

"Not really, just haven't made the effort to talk to her much. Besides, it was kinda tacky." I can't believe Emily's still on speaking terms with both of them, that she invited them last night. If I were her I wouldn't want to see either of them ever again.

"It really was," she nods. "For both of them. I think I told her that last night as well."

"It certainly was an eventful night, wasn't it?"

"Oh! I haven't told you the other thing. Sarah and Shane had a massive fight. It was after you went to bed. He was flirting with that girl - ah, what's her name? She's got blonde hair, she's in the band . . ."

"Caroline?"

"Caroline! That's it. Anyway, they were flirting - well, she was flirting, he was listening, Sarah gets annoyed, and they start arguing. Meanwhile the rest of us are just standing there, trying to look as if we're *not* watching with bated breath to see what they'll do next."

"Did they make up?"

"I don't think so."

I'll have to go and talk to her later. As soon as possible. Only I don't know if she'll want to see me . . .

I hate fighting with her. We never fight. We've had minor rows that last ten minutes and then we hug and apologise profusely, and everything's OK again. But never like this. Never yelling at each other, and storming out.

After I finish my tea I tell Emily I have to get home. I hug her, Roisín, Barry, and assorted people whose names have deserted me, and leave.

My parents are waiting for me.

"Where have *you* been?"

Chapter Seventy-Five

"I left you a note," I say.

"We were in the house, Abigail. Why didn't you tell us you were going out?"

"Because you wouldn't have let me." That's true. They're not a fan of last-minute arrangements. In fact, they despise them. They like to plan ahead, have time to get phone numbers and addresses and probably police records while they're at it.

"I'm starting to think we *shouldn't* let you out if you're going to behave like this." Ah, parent-logic.

"I'm going upstairs," I say.

"Not until you tell us where you were."

I sigh in exasperation. "I left you a note. I told you I was going over to Emily's."

"And who is this Emily? You've never mentioned her before."

I thought I was past the stage of my parents keeping tabs on every single person I hang around with. Clearly not.

"She's a friend," I say.

"Where does she live?"

I give them the address.

"And you stayed at her house last night?"

"Yes." I honestly don't see the point of all this.

"Without telling us in advance?"

How many times do I have to say it? "I left you a note!"

"Don't yell at us."

"So *listen* to me! I left you a note, I'm home now, and I'm going up to my room."

"We'd just like to know where you are. What if there was an emergency?"

"Then call my mobile!" I yell down at them.

"There was no answer."

"I had it switched on. Are you going to start

blaming me for the bad coverage now, too?"

"You need to let us know if you're going to be going out."

"I did!" Are they stupid or something?

"No address, no number . . ."

"Well, you have them now. Good for you. Now you can keep a close eye on me at all times and make sure I *never* have any fun." I go into my room and slam the door. Then I scream. I can't remember the last time I screamed, if ever. It makes me feel a little better.

Chapter Seventy-Six

After I shower and get changed, I go downstairs.

"Can I go over to Sarah's?" I ask the parents politely.

They exchange looks. I can tell they're thinking, *Should we let her out or make her suffer?*

"Be back for dinner," my dad finally says. I'm glad. The last thing I needed was to be grounded. Parents don't care if you absolutely *need* to see your friend because she's upset. As far as they're concerned, it's not important. We're only children, after all. I hate it.

My heart is pounding as I walk down to her house. I don't want another fight.

Sarah's looking out of her bedroom window. She sees me. I freeze. She runs downstairs and opens the door to me.

"Hey," she half-smiles.

"Hey," I say. "I'm sorry."

She nods. "Me too." She hugs me tightly. "I'm sorry . . . I shouldn't have been such a bitch to you."

"It's OK. You weren't. I was just - being me. Being horrible."

"You're not, you're not!"

We head up to her room. "I heard about your fight with Shane," I say quietly.

"Ah, yes. *That* was fun," she mutters sarcastically.

"What happened, exactly?"

"He was flirting with Caroline. I got annoyed. He said I was overreacting, and that *really* pissed me off, since he gets unbelievably jealous if I so much as *look* at another guy."

"It's pretty unreasonable," I agree.

"And then he left, and I left, and that was that. I haven't talked to him since."

"Are you going to?"

"I don't know. I want to, but I'm still really angry with him." She sighs. "Anyway. Did you hear about what Roisín said to Fiona?"

"Yeah, Roisín told me this morning."

"This morning? Where'd you see her?"

"Oh, a few of us stayed the night at Emily's."

"Ah. I see." She pauses. "So, you seem to be getting pretty close to Emily . . ."

"Oh, you noticed that too?" I grin.

She laughs. "Got anything you want to tell me, Abi?"

"We're friends. That's it," I shrug.

"That's not what the guys were saying," she grins. "I think you two made their night. What is it with guys and their obsession with seeing two girls together?"

"I think it's more that they want to join in," I surmise.

She laughs. Everything's back to normal, we're friends again, and all is as it should be.

Chapter Seventy-Seven

Sarah and I spend the afternoon discussing other people's love lives. We return to the subject of Fiona and Hugh.

"I know she liked him, but I still can't believe the fact that she went after someone else's boyfriend," Sarah frowns.

"In fairness, though, he made it really obvious he was interested in her," I point out.

"True," she nods. "They're both to blame, I guess. Still - it's really not like Fiona to do something like this."

"I guess you never really know some people," I say.

"The words 'pot', 'kettle' and 'black' come to mind," she says pointedly.

"There's not much to know about me," I tell her. "You know all the important things."

She seems doubtful. "Can I read some of your poems sometime?"

"What?"

"Please?"

"If you really want to . . . but they're horribly, horribly self-indulgent. They're awful."

"Pleeeease?" she begs.

"OK," I smile.

"Yay. Thank you."

"But you're going to be sorry . . ." I warn her.

She rolls her eyes. "Stop putting yourself down."

"It's an addiction."

"So get help."

"I don't think there is any."

"Sure there is. You've got me, for a start, haven't you?" she grins.

Yeah. I guess I do.

Chapter Seventy-Eight

As promised, I'm home for dinner. While we eat I'm thinking about Shane. I'm still a little attracted to him, still mildly infatuated with him. Even though I think he acted like an asshole towards Sarah, I still like him.

But only a little. I can deal with it. I can fantasise about him but not be crazily madly passionately in love with him. It's a good way to be, I guess, and yet oddly unfulfilling. I miss the craziness, even if it hurts.

"I hate fish," Jess complains. "Why do we have to eat it?"

"It's Good Friday," my mom reminds her.

"So?" she moans. "I don't care."

"Eat your dinner. It's good for you."

"You're not making us go to Mass on Sunday, are you?"

One look from Mom tells her that yes, yes she is making us go.

Jess whines. Greg joins in. I leave the table and go watch *The Simpsons* and wonder what poems to let Sarah read.

Chapter Seventy-Nine

I don't see Sarah until after the weekend. She comes over on Tuesday and we rent out videos and munch on popcorn.

"Shane and I talked," she says.

"And?"

"And we made up," she beams.

She's so happy. It hurts a little, but it's OK. I can handle it.

I go into the kitchen to get more Coke. The knives look so tempting. I pick one up. I'm not sad or angry or depressed - I'm OK, and still I pick one up. Habit, I guess.

The door begins to open and I put it back quickly.

I think about it that night. Is it just a matter of picking up a bad habit and not being able to stop? Would I have used it if I hadn't been interrupted or would I have put it back anyway?

Do I perhaps think too much about this little occupation of mine and blow it out of all proportions? Maybe.

I curl up with a book that night and stay up until two reading. I haven't done that in ages. My childhood solace, and I've been neglecting it, abandoning it for parties and moping. There's something so delightfully comforting about being wrapped up in a duvet with your eyes glued to the page of an interesting book. It feels safe.

There is a razor-blade in the drawer beside my bed, and I don't touch it once all night. It's a start.

Chapter Eighty

Back into the blue monstrosity on Monday morning. I look at my reflection with disgust. What were they thinking when they designed this uniform? Were they actually trying to make us look as hideous as possible?

I think of my school and realise that the answer is probably yes. I can picture the scene. There's a group of teachers sitting around a conference table - or perhaps a cauldron - cackling evilly, plotting fiendishly to come up with an utterly revolting school uniform.

I walk into my classroom and leave my bag beside my chair. The usual group is over at one side of the room chatting. I get out my books as I debate whether or not to go over there. I listen to what they're talking about, and - oh, I don't believe this.

"You know Emily Keating in Fifth Year? She was at this party and met some girl. In front of everyone, like!" Gosh, you don't say . . .

"Seriously? God. I'm not homophobic or anything, but - she doesn't need to shove it in everyone's faces, you know?" Of course not. She should be hiding in a closet somewhere, afraid to show her face, right?

"Yeah, I'd be freaked out by that," Karen says.

I feel like I'm in some kind of parody. I simply can't believe they're for real. It's too much to even get me annoyed or offended or anything like that. I just can't take any of them seriously any more. They don't matter.

The bell goes to signal the start of the first class and they start moving, getting their books. I'm glad. I don't think I could take another two minutes of their inane rambling.

I go up to the Fifth Years at breaktime. Sarah and Fiona aren't in their classroom. I peek into Emily's and see them in there.

Sarah, Emily, Roisín and Fiona are sitting together. "Hey," they greet me, almost simultaneously.

"Hey," I say. I look at Emily and feign shock. "I heard you were with some girl at this party over Easter."

She rolls her eyes. "Oh, I don't believe this. They're gossiping about me in Fourth Year too?"

"The people in this school are pretty pathetic," Sarah reminds her.

"No kidding," she says. She doesn't seem that bothered by it all, though. I figured she wasn't the type to care what other people think, but it's still a relief to know that she isn't upset that everybody's talking about her.

If everyone was talking about me - which they are in a way, I guess, only they don't know it's me - would I be that at ease? I find myself wondering. I tell myself I wouldn't care, that I don't care what those idiots think of me, but I'm not sure. It's hard to be whispered about and not to let it affect you.

Roisín opens up a bag of crisps and offers them around. Fiona refuses one. "No thanks, I've been told I'm kind of fat," she kids.

"Hey, I said I was sorry," Roisín says, putting on a sad face. "Forgive me? Please?"

Fiona grins. "Of course. But I still don't want one."

"Well, on behalf of Mr Tayto, I feel very rejected."

"Don't tell me you're actually on a diet," Sarah says.

"Do I look crazy?" Fiona responds. "God, that'd be almost as bad as . . ."

"Exercising," I suggest.

"Exactly! Insane!"

We're still continuing with this when the bell goes for the end of break. I don't want to leave.

"See you at lunch-time," Sarah says.

I find myself bemoaning the fact that classes are getting in the way of my socialising as I return to my own class. Hmmm . . . something's wrong with *this* picture . . .

Chapter Eighty-One

"Abi, are you going out for lunch?" Karen asks.

"Yeah, probably," I respond, wondering why she's asking. Hannah and Leanne must be busy.

"Going to the shop?"

"Probably."

"Can I walk down with you?"

"Sure, Karen," I say sweetly. "You can walk down with me, and Sarah, and Fiona, and Emily, and while you're at it you can tell her that you're freaked out by her."

"You're friends with her?"

"Yes, I'm friends with her."

"Sorry . . . I didn't know."

"So that makes it OK?"

"You know what I mean."

"No, I don't. I saw your face this morning when Tina told you about Emily meeting a girl. You were completely disgusted."

"Look, it just makes me uncomfortable, OK?"

"Why? Sounds like externalised self-hatred, if you ask me."

She stares at me blankly for a moment before her

mind comprehends. "I'm not a lesbian," she says with obvious distaste.

"It's not an insult, Karen. It's not even a big deal."

"Oh, and I suppose you were there, *completely* comfortable with it."

"With what?" I feign ignorance.

"With Emily kissing another girl!" she says in exasperation.

"That didn't happen," I tell her. "She didn't kiss the girl. The girl kissed her."

"How would you know?"

I look at her for a moment. "How do you think, Karen?"

Her jaw drops. The look on her face is absolutely priceless.

"So you don't want to walk down to the shop with us at lunch-time, then?" I ask innocently.

Chapter Eighty-Two

Shane and Barry are waiting outside the school at lunch-time. When we walk out, some blonde girl (with obvious dark roots) is throwing herself at Shane.

"Hi, Wendy," Sarah says pointedly.

Ah. So this is Wendy. Why am I not surprised?

Shane puts his arm around Sarah. "Will we go?"

He nods to Wendy. "Nice talking to you," he says politely, then whispers something to Sarah. She giggles.

"What are you guys doing here?" Emily asks as we start walking.

"Half-day," Barry explains. "Thought we'd come down here and rub it in your faces."

"How kind," Emily says.

We go down to the shop and hang around there. Sarah and Shane are being their usual couple-ish selves. We pretend they don't exist and leave them to their own devices. I decide I want to buy a drink, after all, and go into the shop. Emily follows me in.

"You OK?" she asks.

"Yeah, I'm OK," I smile.

"Not too upset about seeing the two of them together?"

"Not really," I say honestly. "I mean, it's not one of my favourite things to see, but it's not that I'm jealous any more. They're just so wrapped up in one another."

"I know. Sickening, isn't it?"

I smile. "Yeah. Hey, I have to ask you something. You remember when we were getting the taxi back to your house, and you said something about Shane being with Sarah to make me jealous?"

"Yeah."

"Was that entirely made up to make me feel better?" I grin.

"Maybe a little," she admits. "I don't know . . . if you hadn't been with Graham that night and if you'd seemed interested in Shane, I think something might have happened. But I don't think he was settling for second-best with Sarah either, you know? He really likes her."

I nod. "Yeah." I pay for my drink and we hover at the entrance of the shop rather than return to the others.

"You know Declan?" I ask.

She nods. "Yeah?"

"You called him an attention-seeker . . ." I trail off. I'm not sure how to ask her whether she really meant it or not.

"Yeah, I know. He got pissed with me about that. But honestly. The guy walks around wearing short-sleeved shirts half the time. The only reason he burns himself is so that people will ask him about it and feel sorry for him."

"Maybe he does it because it helps him deal with . . . I don't know, whatever he's going through. You can't just judge him like that."

"Oh, believe me, I can and I will. I've known the guy for years. He can be nice at times, which is why I'm still friends with him, but he spends most of his time moaning to anyone who'll listen. Kind of like

Graham, I suppose."

"Maybe he has a reason to moan," I suggest.

"Abi!" she says in exasperation. "Just trust me on this. Even if he has his reasons, that's no excuse. He's completely self-absorbed. You can't talk to him about your own life because he'll start complaining about his own. Or he starts oh-so-casually rolling up his sleeve so you'll ask him how he got those scars. Don't feel sorry for him."

"I can just understand how he feels," I say.

"You're nothing like him," she says quietly.

"How do you know?"

"Because you keep *your* scars hidden. You don't want people to worry about you. You see people like Declan and Graham and they sicken you, and you don't want to be like that. You just want to feel better."

I stare at her. "How did -"

"I noticed them at the party."

"I wasn't going to ask that. I mean, how do you know all that?"

She shrugs. "I can be perceptive from time to time."

"No kidding." Maybe she's right and maybe she isn't. Either way, I like her interpretation better than mine.

Stereotype

Chapter Eighty-Three

We return to the group. "We came up with a name for the band," Shane announces.

"About time!" Emily says.

"Insert Title Here," he says.

"That's . . . a total cop-out," she laughs. "But cool. I like it."

"What d'you think, Abi?" he asks me. His eyes meet mine for a moment. Nothing. I'm over him.

"It's cool," I nod in agreement.

We walk back to the school. I'm quiet. Thinking. Thinking about what Emily said, mostly. I still feel like I am one of those people, one of the self-absorbed brats like Graham and Declan. I want to shock people. Isn't that why I kissed Emily? Isn't that why I told Karen about it? I want to be outrageous. Nothing more outrageous than that in an all-girls school.

But it's not who I am. I shouldn't have done it. I know I shouldn't have, I knew two minutes later that I shouldn't have.

And then there's another part of me that did it to feel wanted. That's what happened with Graham, too. I think of him and it makes me feel almost physically sick. I imagine kissing him - oh, *oh*. What was I *thinking*? The guy *repels* me.

I need to stop doing that, need to stop using people to make myself feel better. That's not who I am, who I want to be. And cutter Abi isn't me, either. I don't want to be one of "them". I never have.

I don't really know who I am any more. I used to be an anti-social misfit. Now I'm - well, hardly the queen of the school, but I feel like I fit in somewhere. What people in my class think of me really doesn't bother me. I have my friends. They're the important ones. I feel - not normal, but happy. Well, maybe that's an exaggeration. Content, then.

I contemplate whether becoming a happy teenager means fitting into another stereotype. No longer the moody whiny adolescent, but the mature, well-adjusted young adult.

That's before I realise that I really don't think anyone in their right mind would describe me as "well-adjusted". Unless someone was holding a gun to their head and forcing them to say that, but since I can't foresee any circumstances in which someone would want to do that . . .

I still don't want to fit into any box, be easily defined as any one thing. Maybe it's not a matter of working at being different. Maybe you just have to be yourself, and everything falls into place after that. I don't know. I guess the only way to find out is to try. Maybe make mistakes along the way, but in the end, you get to where you want to be. I hope . . .

THE END